His green eyes roved over her hungrily

"Last night," he said, "after I left you lying there so helplessly—I know it was a game, but let me finish—you stayed in my mind, haunting my thoughts. By morning, I was nearly convinced I'd conjured you up out of my jet lag."

Gaelle stared at him in wonder. After the others in her party had gone down to the saloon to discuss the mystery, she had remained in her room, wondering about him, too. But she'd had no jet lag to confuse her. The image of him, framed in her doorway like an avenging angel, had stayed with her, so real that she awoke hot and clammy from dreaming about him.

He saw the wonder in her eyes. "You felt it, too, didn't you?"

"Yes...."

VALERIE PARV had a busy and successful career as a journalist and advertising copywriter before she began writing for Harlequin in 1982. She is an enthusiastic member of several Australian writers' organizations. Her many interests include her husband, her cat and the Australian environment. Her love of the land is a distinguishing feature in many of her books for Harlequin. She has recently written a colorful study in a non-fiction book titled *The Changing Face of Australia*. Her home is in New South Wales.

VALERIE PARV

man without a past

Harlequin Books

TORONTO • NEW YORK • LONDON
AMSTERDAM • PARIS • SYDNEY • HAMBURG
STOCKHOLM • ATHENS • TOKYO • MILAN

Harlequin Presents first edition December 1989
ISBN 0-373-11229-7

Original hardcover edition published in 1988
by Mills & Boon Limited

CHAPTER ONE

IF THEY were going to murder her, Gaelle Maxwell wished they would hurry up and get it over with. The guesthouse was heated, but evenings could be chilly in the Blue Mountains, and, with the french doors to her room wide open on to the balcony, she was shivering in her silky nightgown.

Trying to make herself more comfortable on the massive brass bedstead, she stretched her arms over her head. With her buttercup-coloured hair streaming down her back in untamed waves and her forget-me-not eyes seductively made-up, she felt like the heroine in a B-grade film. No doubt she looked the part, too. Why had she allowed Krys to talk her into this?

Hundreds of underprivileged children would benefit from this weekend, she reminded herself, recalling her friend Krys's assurance. It was worth a little suffering on Gaelle's part.

A rustling sound on the balcony caught her attention, and foolishly, she began to feel nervous. What if something went wrong?

'It isn't going to,' she told herself firmly. Krys knew what she was doing.

Then the man was in her room and there was no more time for thinking, only for reacting. That part was easy. As soon as she caught sight of the wickedly curved blade in his upraised hand, she began to scream in earnest.

'That's it—louder!' the man urged, bending over her.

Feeling her throat becoming raw, Gaelle gulped a breath of air. 'You're enjoying this, aren't you?'

He smiled, his teeth flashing in the moonlight spilling from the balcony. 'You bet! It isn't often I get to bump off a delectable young lady by invitation.'

'Well, get on with it!' she spat out, her nerves taut despite her assurance to herself. 'I haven't got all night.'

'You haven't even got the next five minutes,' he vowed, and raised the knife again, plunging it downwards.

Seeing the blade arcing towards her, Gaelle felt real fear. Had he gone mad? Her screams became chillingly convincing.

Suddenly they were blinded by the glare of the room lights and the knife was wrenched from the man's hand, to go flying across the room. Paralysed with shock, Gaelle watched as her attacker was thrown bodily into the opposite corner, where he lay like a rag doll, too winded to speak.

'Are you all right?'

Gaelle looked up into a pair of malachite-green eyes which were as hard as their mineral namesake. The face which framed them could have been carved from granite too. It was all sharply chiselled angles under a thatch of close-cropped black hair. 'Who are you?' she asked.

'Skip the social niceties. Luckily I got here before that maniac carved you up, but I'd better call the police before he comes around.'

Looking at Roger still crumpled in the corner, Gaelle realised that her gallant rescuer didn't have a clue what was going on. As he made for the door she struggled upright. 'No, wait! It isn't what you think.'

He swung around, his expression grim. 'You aren't one of those women who goes in for kinky sex, are you?'

Violently she shook her head. 'No, I'm not. Oh, for goodness' sake, stop looking so vengeful and sit down here!' She patted the edge of the bed. 'We're all playing a game this weekend. Didn't anybody tell you?'

He picked up the knife and hefted it in one hand, then let it drop on to the dresser where it clanked ominously against the wash basin. He came back to her bedside, but made no move to sit down. 'Whatever you were playing, it was a pretty dangerous game, lady. That knife is very real.'

'I know. But it isn't, honestly. It's all part of a murder mystery weekend being staged here to raise money for charity. I'm surprised you could be staying here and not know what was going on.'

He fixed her with a hard stare. 'I came up here for a quiet weekend on the invitation of a friend. He must have known what was planned, and didn't see fit to enlighten me.'

'Maybe he didn't think you would come,' ventured Gaelle, remembering her own reluctance. Only loyalty to Krys and her good causes had persuaded her. And even then, she had elected to be the murder victim, knowing that her part would be over quickly, allowing her to enjoy the best of the weekend to herself while the other guests tried to solve the mystery.

'I certainly wouldn't have come,' the man said shortly. 'I have no time for stupid games.'

'There's no need to be uppity about it,' Gaelle retorted hotly, annoyed by the man's arrogance. 'There's nothing wrong with letting one's hair down occasionally, or haven't you heard the old saying about all work and no play?'

The man's green eyes lightened fractionally. 'So you think I'm a dull boy, do you?'

His inspection made her acutely conscious of the scantiness of her attire. The nightdress was made of sheer fabric and had a centre-slit bodice with a double-tiered skirt which ended in a handkerchief hemline. Gaelle had been thrilled to discover it in secondhand clothing store, and had lovingly trimmed it with her own handmade lace. It was ideal for a swooning murder victim, but barely decent for entertaining a strange man in her bedroom.

She resisted the urge to pull the eiderdown over herself. It was a bit late for that. 'I wouldn't know what sort of man you are, dull or otherwise. We still have to introduced.'

He offered his hand and was about to say something, presumably his name, when there was a groan from the corner of the room. Gaelle leapt up and ran to Roger's side, helping him to his feet. 'Are you all right, Roger?'

Roger nodded groggily and let her help him to the bed, where he sat down heavily. Then he noticed the other man standing at the end of the bed, and tensed.

'Don't hit me, I'm not an intruder,' he said quickly.

'So your girlfriend assures me. Look, I'm sorry if I

barged in at the wrong moment, but I was walking down the corridor when I heard screams. From where I stood, it looked as if you were about to . . .'

'Bump her off?' Roger cut in. 'I was—but only for the purpose of a mystery weekend.'

'I understand that now,' the stranger said curtly. 'So I'll leave you to your entertainment. Goodnight.'

'Wait!' Gaelle said urgently, realising that she hadn't thanked him for saving her life, which he had believed he was doing. But the stranger was gone.

Roger looked after him speculatively. 'Funny bloke wasn't he? I'm surprised he didn't know about the weekend. Krys said we'd be the only people staying here.'

'He's a friend of a friend. And apparently the friend didn't think to warn him,' she observed. She was well aware that the stranger had mentally paired her off with Roger, and for some reason that thought bothered her.

There hadn't been time to explain that Roger was Krys's brother-in-law. His wife, Carrie—Krys's sister—was here this weekend, along with another dozen people who thought it would be fun spending the weekend trying to catch the murderer. Krys had reasoned that a celebrated cartoonist like Roger Torkan would be the most unlikely murderer. Gaelle turned to him in concern, remembering that he had nearly been the victim instead. 'Are you sure you're all right?' she asked anxiously.

'I'm fine. Your knight in shining armour only winded me when he threw me against the wall.' He flexed his shoulders experimentally. 'Whoever he is, he packs a wallop!'

'Still, he'd be good to have around if you were really being murdered,' Gaelle observed, her gaze shifting to the door where the stranger had stood moments before. He was so tall and broad, quite the most impressive man she'd encountered in a long time. And those eyes! She felt a wave of heat wash over her where not so long ago she'd been shivering. Who was he and what was he doing here?

It was an effort to dismiss him from her mind so that she could go on playing her role. When the others came to inspect the body, as planned, a short time later, they had no idea how busy were the thoughts of the corpse as she lay decoratively across the bedstead, her lovely gown stained with red. She was trying to work out how she could get out of this and find her would-be rescuer. At least she owed him her thanks for doing what he had thought was the right thing.

But, more than that, she burned to know more about him and what brought him to Megalong. If it wasn't a murder, what was it?

CHAPTER TWO

THE MORNING mist over the Megalong Valley had lifted to reveal an afternoon of sparkling beauty. Careful not to crush her oyster-coloured silk dress, Gaelle relaxed on a garden bench with her back to the circular driveway, facing the croquet lawns and the sweep of the valley beyond.

She was glad she hadn't gone with the other guests on their picnic, during which Krys would lead them to some judiciously placed clues. Gaelle had insisted that it wasn't proper for the murder victim to go along, secretly welcoming the chance of the afternoon to herself. She would rejoin the others at dinner when she was to haunt the dining-room in what Krys termed her Lady Macbeth scene. The dress, another of her thrift-shop finds, added to the atmosphere. Like the other guests, she had dressed in keeping with the weekend.

'For a corpse, you look remarkably beautiful!'

She caught her breath in surprise as she looked up into the eyes of her mystery man. In daylight, he looked even more prepossessing. Measuring his height against the spear-topped, wrought-iron fence, she judged him to be over six feet tall, with broad shoulders and chest, tapering to lean hips and well-muscled legs which strained the grey canvas of his trousers. His wide-apart stance with his hands

11

planted on hips suggested a confidence bordering on arrogance. If it wasn't for the shadows clouding the malachite eyes, she would have thought he owned the world.

'I didn't hear you coming,' she said fatuously, annoyed that she couldn't think of anything more original.

'I'm quiet on my feet. Look, I wanted to apologise for the way I acted last night.'

So he had been looking for her. The idea gave her a curious thrill. 'There's no need to apologise,' she assured him. 'I should thank you, in fact. You were brave to come barging in like that, not knowing the attack was staged.'

He raked a hand through his dark hair. 'Barging in is right! I haven't felt so foolish since college.'

'You weren't foolish. You did what you thought was right. But don't worry, Roger and I won't say anything.' Gaelle smiled. 'He has to establish an alibi and I'm supposed to be dead!'

His answering smile evoked a tingling sensation within her, as if he had touched her physically, instead of only with his gaze. 'I repeat—for a corpse, you look very beautiful.'

She felt her colour heightening and hated the way she knew it made her freckles stand out against her alabaster skin. She dipped her head. 'You're very gallant, kind sir.'

'No, just observant. You *are* beautiful. Is that dress some sort of costume?'

Smoothing the gown between her fingers, she nodded. 'I'm Lady Victoria Gaynor, daughter of the house.' She gestured behind them, indicating

Megalong, then lowered her voice. 'I was cruelly done in by the wicked Sir Roger Marchant because I refused to marry him and solve all his financial worries with my dowry.'

He fell into the spirit of the game. 'The cad! I should have had it out with him last night.'

'Don't worry, he'll be caught soon enough. Krys. . . er . . . The countess Krystine . . . doesn't believe in subtle clues,' she said, laughing, then added, 'And who, prithee, are you?'

He thought for a moment. 'I'm the Honourable Peter Ridge, unacknowledged scion of a noble family.'

Gaelle stood up and curtsied low. 'Delighted to meet you, sir.'

He lifted her hand and kissed the back of it, his breath warm and teasing against her skin. 'Enchanted, Lady Victoria.'

'My name is really Gaelle Maxwell,' she confided, abandoning her character. She waited expectantly.

'You can call me Pete.' He glanced at the book open beside her on the garden bench. 'I'd better leave you to your reading.'

Suddenly Gaelle felt the need to keep him with her. 'Don't go. I was just passing the time until the others come back.'

On the point of returning to the house, he hesitated. He seemed torn between the desire to go and the urge to stay, like a wild stag who was tempted by the offer of food, yet wary of the one who had offered it. 'I take it the others are still on the murder trail?'

She nodded. 'They'll be away until tea-time.' Now

why had she told him that? She was almost afraid to examine her motives too closely, so she hurried on, 'Are you a friend of Krys Doyle's?'

'I met her for the first time when I arrived. She seems very young to own a place like this.'

Letting her gaze rove over the acres of ground with their towering stands of pines and eucalypts, Gaelle inclined her head in agreement. 'Krys's mother owned Megalong originally, and built it up from a rundown mansion into a successful guesthouse. She put it on the market to return to her estranged husband. After growing up here. Krys couldn't bear to part with it, so she bought it without telling her mother where the money came from. Otherwise her mother would have given Krys the house, and she needed the proceeds to live on.'

Pete seemed uninterested in this information. 'So where do you fit in?' he asked.

'I went to school with Krys and we kept in touch, although she dropped out to become an artist. She's very successful.'

'I thought I'd heard of her. Are you an artist too?'

'Good grief, no! I'm a genealogist—I specialise in tracing people's family trees. The only artistic thing I do is sew.'

'Did you make that thing you were wearing last night?' he asked.

Surprised but pleased to find he remembered, she nodded.

'Yes—at least, some of it. The gown is an antique, but I made the lace trimmings.'

'Pity it had to end up bloodstained. You looked enchanting in it, like something out of a dream.'

The trite phrase could have sounded shallow and empty, but he said it in a wistful away, as if she represented something he had been looking for all his life. Gaelle looked at him speculatively, expecting him to add some comment which would spoil the illusion. But he kept silent, his eyes fixed on the far peaks.

'What brings you here, Pete?' she asked, a little breathlessly.

He came out of his trance abruptly. 'I just got back from London and needed somewhere to banish my jet lag. This seemed like the ideal place.'

Involuntarily, she laughed. 'Except that you picked the wrong weekend. You said a friend invited you. Was it Carrie Torkan?'

'What makes you think so?'

'She acts as her husband's agent, and his cartoons are syndicated in London. I thought you might be involved.'

His green eyes rested on her thoughtfully. 'You're playing the wrong role this weekend. You should have been the detective instead of the victim!'

So she was right about his connections with the Torkans. She should have been pleased, but his answer only fuelled her desire to know more about him. 'Are you from Sydney?' she asked.

'Melbourne, he answered shortly. 'I have a house in Sydney, but a friend uses it. I have a home in London too. Would you like to know my annual salary?'

Shocked, she stared at him. 'Of course not! I wasn't prying. All right, maybe I was. But my business is knowing people, so curiosity is an occupational hazard.'

He let his breath out in a hissing sigh. 'I'm sorry, I was being overly sensitive—bad habit of mine. I don't even have your excuse. Am I forgiven?'

The lop-sided smile with which he favoured her did unsettling things to her stomach. 'Yes, you are—if I'm forgiven for poking my nose into your affairs. I promise not to ask any more questions, all right?'

'It's a deal.' He hesitated a moment, agonising over some internal decision which he reached in a rush. 'Maybe we can make it up to each other by having lunch together. You said the others won't be back for a while.'

'I know, but . . .'

'You have other plans?' he intervened. 'I should have realised. Your friend Roger must be taking you somewhere.' His tone was oddly flat, as if with disappointment.

'It's nothing like that,' Gaelle told him. 'Roger is Carrie's husband. I'm surprised you two haven't met, if you do business with her.'

'I do most of my business overseas,' he explained. 'I haven't been back to Australia for months.'

'I see.'

'Well, what about lunch, then?'

'Yes.' She couldn't explain, even to herself, the mixture of feelings Pete evoked in her. Somehow he managed to attract and repel her all at once. She was intrigued by his air of self-possession, charmed by his humour and warmth, yet held at bay by his air of mystery. He reminded her of an Irish wolfhound: large, lean and gentle in appearance, but perfectly capable of savaging an innocent sheep.

They want to a restaurant only a short walk away from Megalong. It was quaintly old-fashioned, with windows overlooking gardens planted with poplar trees. The view stretched on to a golf course and a rainforest glen beyond.

By the time they had consumed a marvellous terrine of duck, followed by rack of lamb with vegetables from the restaurant's garden, Pete had learned a lot about Gaelle, from the fact that she lived alone in an Edwardian terrace house in Clontarf left to her by her father, to her passion for lacemaking. At the same time, she realised she knew no more about him than she had when they started the meal.

'You don't talk about yourself much, do you?' she asked as they walked back to Megalong.

'I would if there was anything to tell.'

'There must be,' she said impatiently. 'For instance, what plays do you like? What's your favourite kind of music?'

'Think of me as Cassius,' he said, sounding as if he was humouring her. ' ''He read much . . . He loves no plays . . . He hears no music.'' '

' ''Seldom he smiles . . . Such men as he be never at heart's ease,'' ' she quoted back, looking at him side-long. 'Are you never at heart's ease?'

'I am now, in your company.' He spoke softly, the mocking tone vanished from his voice.

'You sound as if you mean it,' she told him.

'I do.' He turned to her suddenly. 'You look so fragile in that Victorian gown, wandering these grounds at my side. Are you sure I'm not dreaming you?'

His voice was vibrant with tightly leashed

emotion. Gaelle wondered how many times he had entrusted his secret needs to dreams because reality was too harsh to nurture them. 'I'm real enough,' she said in a low voice.

His green eyes roved over her hungrily and he clasped her upper arms. 'Last night, after I left you lying there so helplessly—I know it was a game, but let me finish—you stayed in my mind, haunting my thoughts. By morning, I was nearly convinced I'd conjured you up out of my jet lag.'

Gaelle stared at him in wonder. After the others had gone down to the saloon to discuss the mystery, she had remained in her room, wondering about him too. The difference was that she'd had no jet lag to confuse her. The image of him, framed in her doorway like an avenging angel, had stayed with her, so real that she awoke hot and clammy from dreaming about him.

He saw the wonder in her eyes. 'You felt it too, didn't you?'

'Yes,'

They looked at each other, shaken by the awareness of powerful forces at work between them. Gaelle felt confused and exhilarated all at once. Nothing like this had ever happened to her before. She was usually so independent, so conservative, thinking every move through before she made it. Yet here she was, admitting to a perfect stranger that the attention he felt for her was mutual.

They had reached the grounds of Megalong, but were shielded from the main building by a thicket of trees. Pete drew her into its shelter. 'You're a most unusual woman, Gaelle,' he told her.

Mesmerised by the intentness of his gaze, she moved closer. 'Am I?'

'You know you are.'

It was as if, by saying it, he made it true. He made her feel special, as if she was the only woman alive. He might be Cassius by the lean and hungry look, but he was also Merlin, able to bewitch her with his eyes. As his face hovered above hers, his eyes as dark as the sea in storm, she felt herself slipping under his spell.

'Gaelle.' He said her name as if it was a poem. 'There's something I want to do.'

She knew what it was. Her was going to kiss her, and she was going to let him. Let him? Every fibre of her being thrilled to the idea. Unconsciously, she parted her lips in invitation.

The pressure of his mouth was warm and firm, evoking a response that made her feel raw inside. She returned his kiss with a passion which alarmed her, discovering a side of her nature she had kept hidden even from herself.

She had certainly never been aware of it while she was going out with Nick Guardino. When she'd refused to give up her career to marry him, he had accused her of wanting to see other men, using that as his excuse to sleep with other women.

Now she knew the fault was Nick's. She had held back from him because she had known he wasn't the right man for her. With Pete, she felt so different. In his arms she felt gloriously, vibrantly alive, as if she had come home at last.

'You know I want you,' he whispered.

After Nick had left her Gaelle had told herself she

wasn't ready for someone new. But that was months ago. Now her body told her that she was ready. Unable to ignore its insistent throbbing, she whispered back, 'I want you, too.'

His arms tightened around her, and she revelled in the strength of his embrace. It was strange. She knew less about him that anyone she had ever dated, far less kissed with such ardour. Yet she knew one thing, and it overrode all else: he was the man for her. She didn't even know what made her so certain, only that she was.

Fleetingly, she remembered her mother describing her first meeting with Gaelle's father. They had been together barely an hour when Gaelle's father had said, 'I shall marry you.' And he had, embarking on nearly thirty years of shared joy until Simpson Maxwell succumbed to a sudden heart attack. Gaelle was the last person to reject the idea of love at first sight;' she had just never dreamed it would happen to her.

She did not resist when Pete guided her on to the springy grass and rested her against his arm, while his free hand explored her body. His hands felt fiery through the silk of her dress, and his hunger for her was increasingly apparent. He needed her, she realised. She had a feeling that he needed her in his life as well.

She could be seeing what she wanted to see in him, she knew, but her intuition had never failed her before. Like her mother, she formed strong first impressions of people. Try as she might to alter them, she was rarely proved wrong on longer acquaintance. I could fall in love with this man, she thought with a sense of wonder.

Could Pete feel it too? He had kissed and caressed her in a way which said he recognised that they belonged together. His caresses heated her limbs until her clothes felt suffocatingly tight and hot. 'Oh, Pete!' she moaned.

'I know, I know.'

He crushed her to him and pushed her dress higher and she drew a strangled breath as his hand claimed each new place at his own. He was every explorer who ever lived, and she was every unexplored continent. The sense of discovery was achingly sweet.

She must be insane, she thought dizzily. How could she behave like this with a man she barely knew? It was as if the word 'no' had been erased from her vocabulary.

Pete's weight shifted suddenly, and she thought he was undressing, until he began to refasten the pearl buttons down the front of her dress. 'What's the matter?' she asked.

'The others are back.'

Only then did the sound of voices intrude on her awareness. She had been so carried away that she hadn't heard Krys's party returning. She felt a crushing sense of loss. 'Oh, no!' she groaned.

Pete's mouth compressed into a tight line. 'It's for the best.'

For whom? Gaelle wanted to think he was worried about what the others would say, but she sensed that he was relieved for himself as well. But what was there to regret? 'You aren't married, are you, Pete?' she asked on a sudden impulse.

'No.'

'Then what's the matter?'

He helped her to her feet and dusted the grass off her back, his touch infuriatingly impersonal. 'Nothing's the matter. I should apologise for getting carried away. If the others hadn't returned . . .'

They would have made love, she finished the thought for him. 'There's no need to apologise,' she assured him aloud. 'I was as responsible as you were.'

'If you can call this responsible,' he said shortly.

As he took a step away from her, she restrained him. 'I have no regrets,' she told him. Except one, she added inwardly, and that was the interruption. He sounded almost glad about it, which made her feel cheap. She didn't like the feeling one bit. 'We both knew what we were doing.'

His thoughtful gaze swept over her. 'I never meant this to happen, Gaelle. Believe me, it's better this way.'

'Wait, please!'

But he was gone, striding towards the house with long steps, as if to put as much distance between them as quickly as he could. She looked after him, feeling angry and tearful by turns. She had nearly given herself to him, sure that her feelings were returned. To find that he was merely 'carried away', and sorry to boot, infuriated her. She felt a childish urge to stamp her foot. How could he just walk away?

He wasn't at dinner, and she couldn't bring herself to discuss him with the other guests, so she stayed moodily silent for most of the meal. Luckily, the others were too busy comparing theories about the identity of the murderer to notice.

When it was time for her to appear as the ghost of the victim, she had to steel herself to play her part. She kept scanning the room, hoping that Pete would appear, yet fearing his response when he did. How would she feel if he was cold and distant; if all the magic between them had been on her side?

Applause shattered her reverie and she realised she had walked through her role, making the moves Krys had rehearsed with her, in a daze. She smiled self-consciously at her audience, then disappeared behind a curtain, to reappear in the hallway moments later. She had planted the last of Krys's clues; now it was up to the others to work out who the murderer was.

As she went wearily up to her room, she heard the arguments start up in the saloon below. They sounded as if they would be there half the night. As their laughter floated up to her, Gaelle envied them their jollity. The strain of waiting for Pete to appear, and wondering how he would react when he did, had left her feeling limp and tired.

On the landing, she hesitated. Megalong had nine guest suites. Which one belonged to Pete? She studied the row of closed doors, mentally ticking off their occupants. Roger and Carrie had the one next to her. On the other side was Krys's celebrity guest, the radio personality Scott Lawson. Gaelle had been introduced to him on the first night. Krys had prevailed on him to lend his name to the weekend and publicise it on his programme. Several couples had come along in response to the publicity, ensuring a substantial donation to the children's charity for whose benefit Krys was staging the event.

Gaelle knew two of the couples by sight. They occupied the suites farthest along the hall from her. That left only the door diagonally opposite her own. The thought that Pete could be behind it at this very moment sent a frisson of excitement down her spine.

Still she wavered. What would he think of her if she simply knocked on his door? She had never done such a thing before. Yet she had never lain in the arms of a stranger until this afternoon.

She was reminded again of her parents, who had known they would marry, after only an hour. They had recognised something special in each other which had endured for thirty years. Gaelle smiled at the memory of her mother, elbow-deep in dishwater, being embraced from behind by Gaelle's father, the two of them laughing like teenagers. This utter certainty that you had found your soulmate could happen. It had happened to Gaelle today. She stepped up to the door and knocked, her heart hammering as loudly as her hand against the polished cedar.

Slowly the door opened and Pete stood framed there. He must have come straight from the shower, because he was dressed only in black jeans slung low on his hips, and his chest glistened with droplets of moisture. His feet were bare. He regarded her incuriously. 'Yes, Gaelle?'

She said the first thing which came into her head. 'I came to say goodnight.'

His green eyes slid over her, and she was surprised by the intensity of the desire she saw in them. Then his lids closed, hooding them. When he looked at her again there was only regret in his expression. 'Goodnight, Gaelle,' he said, with such weariness that she knew she couldn't desert him in such a bleak mood.

Hardly aware of what she was doing, she slid her arms around his neck and pressed against the warmth of his chest. 'I meant properly.'

All resistance fled and his arms closed around her. 'Dear God, Gaelle! Just remember I warned you.'

He had warned her, but he hadn't forewarned her. When he led her into his room and closed the door, she knew a door was closing on part of her life as well. Where the future led, she could only sense.

As he slid her clothes off, item by item, her skin glowed with a fiery warmth which cool mountain air couldn't quench. Only Pete could do that, but relief was not yet. Oh, no, not yet.

When her wispy briefs and bra were all that shielded her from his inspection, he touched the delicate lace trimmings with a teasing finger. 'Very nice!'

'I made them myself,' she told him, her voice vibrant with barely contained longing.

'Clever girl,' he murmured, sliding his hand inside the bra. 'Is there no end to your talents?'

His fingers found her sensitive nipple and teased it to pert expectancy. Her breathing quickened and she placed her own hand over his, pressing him to her. 'What about you? What are your special talents?'

He proceeded to show her, taking her breath away altogether as he drove her to heights of sensation she had only imagined. Surely her heart couldn't sustain such frantic beating? Already she thought he must hear it pounding in time with the ebb and flow of their passion. She began to call his name over and over.

When iron control was no longer enough, Pete joined with her in a crescendo that swept them irresistibly on to joyous release. She heard him crying her name as he held her fiercely to him, their breathing mingling into one great, gasping sigh of shared discovery.

Then they were coasting down the other side of the mountain, their tandem heartbeats slowing at last. Gaelle felt the breath returning to her body, and the night air felt cool on her heated skin. She looked at Pete in amazement. 'My God!' she gasped.

'I know.' He wiped the damp strands of hair back from her forehead. 'I was mad to think I could just walk away from you this afternoon.'

'Why did you want to?'

He propped himself up on one elbow. 'I didn't want to. It was the last thing I wanted, in fact. But I thought I was doing the right thing.'

'And now?'

'Honest to God, I don't know. I wish I did.'

Baffled, Gaelle turned her head away. She wasn't sure what she had expected him to say, but it wasn't that. Surely he didn't intend to walk out of her life now, knowing the strength of the attraction which existed between them? 'It isn't only sex, you know,' she said.

She felt him change even before she saw his shoulder muscles go rigid as he turned his back to her. 'So what if it is?' he snapped. 'There's nothing wrong with what we just shared.'

'Unless that's all there is.' Moments ago, everything had felt so right between them. She knew he had felt it too.

She swung her legs over the side of the bed and reached for her underslip. Pete remained silent as she dressed. He was still sitting on the edge of the bed, unmoving, when she finished. Hands on hips, she confronted him. 'I don't understand you,' she told him.'

He looked up, his eyes hooded and unreadable. 'I'm not asking you to understand me. I gave you what I thought you wanted.'

'What I wanted? You make it sound so cheap! I know it was more than that. There was something special between us—we both felt it as soon as we met.'

'And we gave in to it,' he said tiredly. 'I'm sorry if I disappointed you.'

'You didn't and you know it!' she swore, her eyes blazing with a combination of anger and humiliation. 'But you have now, with your attitude!'

Snatching up her shoes, she made for the door. Her hand was resting on the knob when Pete said, 'Gaelle, wait!'

But she didn't want to hear any more platitudes or assurances from him. She wrenched the door open and flung herself across the corridor to her own room.

In its sanctuary, she leaned against the door and let the sobs come. There were no tears, just great, racking tremors of pain and anguish. What an idiot she was! It was bad enough to have thrown herself at him on the strength of an imagined attraction, but to

have him treat it as no more than satisfied lust made
her feel hideously cheap. Shedding her clothes again,
she turned the shower on full blast and let it sluice
away any traces of his touch and her tears. There was
no way she could face him tomorrow, knowing what
he thought.'I warned you,' he had said. She should
have heeded his warning. Now she had no choice.
She decided to leave tomorrow, before the others
came down to breakfast, making some excuse to
Krys. She had been a fool, but only the two of them
knew it, and she didn't intend to see him again.

CHAPTER THREE

AVOIDING Pete was easier than getting him out of her mind, Gaelle discovered. Nearly a month had gone by since the mystery weekend, but he still intruded on her thoughts at the most unexpected times.

When she rummaged through her wardrobe and her hand brushed the oyster silk dress, she was walking beside him again through the grounds of Megalong. Pressing the antique nightgown, which had cleaned easily, after all, she was back in her bedroom, seeing Pete framed in her doorway, his eyes flashing fire at Roger for threatening her. The mere whiff of citrus was enough to flood her senses with evocations of his aftershave lotion, imprinted on her mind from the moment when they made love. It was as if her love had died, leaving her a host of memories.

It *had* died, she told herself crossly. Died a-borning, if she was honest with herself. She was the only one who had felt the tug of attraction. To Pete, she was just a casual sexual conquest, probably forgotten by now. If she had any sense, she would do the same, instead of nursing fantasies about what might have been.

She still had difficulty accepting that she had allowed a total stranger to make love to her at Megalong. Allowed him? What a joke! She had been a more-than-willing participant. The memory made her cheeks burn. How could she have behaved like that?

She pressed her palms against her burning cheeks. It had happened. She would have to accept it, forgive herself and go on from there.

Luckily she had plenty of work to distract herself. She was in the middle of wrestling with her microfiche reader, trying to establish whether the Beale she sought had been misspelled in the 1837 census as Baillie, a common occurence which hampered researchers like herself.

Cross-checking proved her right, and she entered the new name in her loose-leaf folder and card index system. Her client, a descendant of Beale-Baillie, would want to know the provenance of her facts.

She was immersed in her talk when the telephone rang. 'Hello?'

'I'm Helen Otford, a researcher on the Scott Lawson radio show,' the caller introduced herself. 'I understand you met Scott at a charity weekend recently?'

Surprised that the famous interviewer had recalled their conversation, Gaelle said, 'I was introduced to him briefly. He was interested in my work as a genealogist.'

'He was more than interested,' Helen replied. 'He asked me to invite you to be interviewed on his programme. Family history is very popular right now.'

A feeling of dread assailed Gaelle. 'It's kind of Mr Lawson to ask me, but I'm not very good at that sort of thing,' she explained.

'I must disagree with you,' said Helen. 'I heard you talk on lacemaking at the evening college, and it was fascinating.'

'That was only to a group of women who wanted to learn the craft. Even then I was so terrified that I was ill before I got up to speak.' Gaelle felt her stomach muscles tighten. Even talking about it made her feel ill. 'I'm sorry, but I have to say no.'

'What a pity!' The researcher sounded genuinely disappointed. 'I don't want you to be upset about it, but would you give it a little thought? We'd love to have you on the show. If anything, it's easier than speaking at the college, because there would only be you and Scott in a cosy studio. You wouldn't know anyone else was listening.'

'You're very persuasive, and I'm flattered that you're so keen to have me. I'll think about it and let you know. All right?'

'Fine. I'll tell Scott what you said.' Helen gave Gaelle her telephone number before saying goodbye.

Staring at the telephone, Gaelle felt her queasiness growing worse. She hadn't felt completely well since the mystery weekend, and the request to appear on Scott Lawson's programme was the final straw. She hated making public appearances, only agreeing to do the talk on lacemaking as a favour to a former teacher of hers. The group had been so friendly and welcoming, and so interested in the craft, that she soon forgot her nerves in her enthusiasm for her subject. But this was different. The Scott Lawson show was a top-rating programme up and down the east coast of Australia. The very idea paralysed her with nerves.

Suddenly she jumped up and bolted for the bathroom as illness overwhelmed her. When she came back, she was white and shaking. Alarmed, she reached for the phone again and telephoned her doctor to make an appointment for a check-up. Nerves alone couldn't account for the way she had been feeling lately.

Her doctor, Jill Barwick, agreed. After giving Gaelle a thorough examination, she leaned back in her swivel chair, her eyes dark with concern. 'Are you still on the pill, Gaelle?'

'Yes—I mean no. That is, I was until Nick and I broke up.'

As a friend as well as her doctor, Jill knew what had happened between Gaelle and Nick Guardino. When asked, she had suggested that Gaelle might be better off with someone who valued her more as a person. With hindsight, Gaelle found that Jill was right. Now the doctor nodded. 'You gave up the pill because you didn't need it any more. It never occurred to you that you might meet someone else.'

Gaelle shook her head. 'Are you trying to tell me I'm pregnant?'

'It looks that way. I'll need the test results to be sure.'

'How long will they take?'

'Normally no time at all, but the lab technicians are on strike, so it'll be a couple of days, I'm afraid.'

Gaelle gave her a wan smile. 'Just my luck!'

'You mean the strike or the pregnancy?'

'Just a minute, Jill,' Gaelle cautioned her, 'I know you think there's no such thing as an accidental pregnancy, but this one is, I promise you.'

Fixing her patient with a knowing look, Jill said, 'Are you quite sure?'

'Of course. I didn't plan this. As it is, I don't know what I'm going to do.'

'Have the baby, I expect,' Jill said smoothly. 'It's what you always wanted.'

Gaelle's eyes widened. 'Yes, it is, isn't it?'

'Still sure it was an accident?'

'My God! Do you think that subconsciously I wanted this to happen?'

'We usually get what we want,' Jill reminded her. 'You've been mad about children, ever since you found out that your mother couldn't have any more after you. If you'd married Nick, you would probably have had his child by now.'

'And no life of my own,' Gaelle said glumly. 'He didn't mind having a family one bit. He just objected to me having a career as well.'

'So you went ahead and solved the problem in your own way.'

'And created a hundred more at the same time,' Gaelle admitted, her mind awhirl with the problems facing her. 'If you're right, I should be thrilled with the news, and I guess I will be when it sinks in. I just wish I'd talked it over with myself first.'

'The mind works in mysterious ways,' Jill observed. 'But don't get too excited yet. Your symptoms point to a pregnancy, but we should wait for the test results.'

'Call me as soon as you know.'

With Jill's promise ringing in her ears, Gaelle walked out of the doctor's office in a daze. She was going to have a baby! She had been so sure her malaise was due to some virus or other, or to nerves brought on by the talk at the college and Helen Otford's call, that she had never considered the alternative. She had simply assumed that, although she had stopped taking the pill, she would be infertile for some time yet.

Her laugh was hysterical enough to make people look at her curiously. How many women had made that mistake? She had never expected to be among them.

Absently she splayed her fingers across her middle, trying to imagine the new life which might already be growing there. In her work, researching the generations of man, she had never felt so keenly how each branch on a family tree led from every other, as inexorably as her child would spring from her.

Thinking of family trees brought another unwelcome thought. On her baby's family tree, what would fill the space where the male line should be? She could fill in his name, Peter Ridge, but that was all. She didn't even know where to start looking for him.

But she was going to try. Now he meant much more to her than a night of uncontrolled desire. He was the father of her child; he had a right to know what had happened.

Thank goodness there was no need to ask him for support. The house belonged to her, and she could work at her own pace. Nor was she concerned about gossip; people could think what they liked. She was more anxious for her child to know its father. In her work, she was saddened by the number of adopted people who came to her, desperate to learn about themselves. She couldn't put her child through such torment.

But was all her concern for the baby? Didn't part of her yearn to see Pete again? This child had been conceived out of a passion that still burned inside her, demanding to be acknowledged. She knew she needed to see him again, for her own sake as well as the baby's.

Telephoning Krys was the obvious first step, but she was saved the necessity when the artist arrived on her doorstep that afternoon, fresh from arranging a new exhibition in the city.

'You look washed out. You must be working too hard,' Krys said sternly, after they had embraced.

Gaelle decided not to enlighten her until the test results confirmed her news. 'I'm fine,' she said dismissively. 'Besides, I just had a weekend off at your place.'

'And earned your keep by being the murder victim,' Krys rejoined.

'I had the easy job, lying around pretending to be dead and haunting the place. Who solved the mystery, by the way?'

'Carrie did,' Krys told her. 'I think Roger would have fooled the others, but his wife knows him too well. She saw right through his alibi.'

'That weekend was a lot of fun, wasn't it?'

'I wasn't sure you thought so, when you insisted on leaving early.'

'I told you, a client wanted to see me urgently.' Gaelle hated lying to Krys, but she was stuck with the tale she had concocted when she'd rushed away from Megalong. She poured coffee for them both, then said as casually as she could, 'I've been meaning to ask you about one of your house guests. I . . . er . . . brought home something of his by mistake, but I don't know his address. His name is Pete Ridge.'

Krys gave her a confused look. 'Pete who?'

In the act of adding cream to their coffee, Gaelle paused. 'Pete Ridge. He works with Carrie in London.'

Krys shook her head. 'Being a murder victim must be getting to you! No one called Ridge was staying at Megalong that weekend.'

'I don't understand. I met him and talked to him.' Among other things, Gaelle added to herself.

'All the same, he wasn't one of my guests—you can check the list yourself. Unless someone on it couldn't come and sent this man to make up the numbers?'

'I don't think so. He didn't seem to know about the murder mystery theme. He mistook Roger's performance for a real attack and rushed in to save me. That's how we met.'

'Roger didn't know him?'

'He didn't seem to,' said Gaelle. 'The man said he'd been invited by a friend.'

'How strange! Maybe he's one of those people who enjoy crashing parties.'

'I don't think so. He was too sure of himself.'

'The best con-men are,' said Krys firmly.

It stung Gaelle to hear Pete described as a con-man. 'He wasn't like that,' she said defensively. 'I know I've heard his name before. It sounded so familiar that he could be someone famous.'

'Or some thing,' Krys supplied. 'It's been nagging at me, too. Now I know where I've seen it—on the drive to the Central Coast. Roger and Carrie have a house at Brooklyn, and whenever I visit them I pass the signs directing you to Peat's Ridge. It's a place, not a person at all.'

A chill feeling swept over Gaelle. Had she been taken in by an expert? 'You're right,' she said in a low voice. 'I've seen the signs myself. How could I have been so stupid?'

Krys regarded her curiously. 'How stupid were you with this man?'

Gaelle took a deep breath. 'About as stupid as one can be.'

'Holey-moley! He must be quite a man!'

There was no censure in Krys's voice, only deep compassion for her friend. Gaelle nodded. 'He is. I really thought we had something special going. But I imagined it, didn't I?'

'Maybe not. I remember when Carrie met Roger, the sparks were there from the first.'

'But at least she knew who he was.' Gaelle's eyes shadowed with misery. 'What am I going to do?'

'Maybe it isn't hopeless,' Krys said thoughtfully. 'There was an extra man at Megalong that weekend, but his name was Dan, not Pete. I don't think he's the one you want, though. He was a guest of Scott Lawson's. They arrived together on the Friday night and left again on Sunday, when Scott was called back to his studio for some emergency or another.'

'I met her for the first time when I arrived.' Pete's comment about Krys replayed itself in Gaelle's mind. Could he have been Scott Lawson's guest? 'Can you describe him?' she asked Krys, and held her breath as she waited for the answer.

'Things were pretty hectic. All I remember is how big the man was—you know, broad shoulders and deep barrel chest, good-looking in a rugged, been-around sort of way.'

Jumping up, Gaelle flung her arms around Krys. 'You're an angel! Can you give me his address?'

''Fraid not. Scott Lawson used his credit card to pay for them both. I don't even have his full name. I suppose you could try the radio station. Getting the great man himself is difficult.' Her mouth twisted as she remembered. 'It took me several calls and a lot of subterfuge to get him to support our weekend. But one of his staff might be able to help you.

Gaelle grinned, relief making her feel light-headed. 'I think I can do better than that!'

She fidgeted through the rest of Krys's visit, torn between enjoying her company and wishing she would leave so that Gaelle could put her idea into action.

At last she was left alone. Her heart began to race as she reached for the phone and she shuddered. This wasn't going to be easy. But it would be worth it if Scott Lawson put her in touch with Pete again.

Or Dan, she corrected herself. Was that his real name? While she waited for the switchboard operator to put her through to Helen Otford, she let Pete/Dan's face fill her mind. Her pulses responded to the image by quickening until she wasn't sure whether her imagination was due to what she was about to do, or to memories of what they had shared.

'Scott Lawson Show, Helen Otford speaking.'

'Hello, Miss Otford, this is Gaelle Maxwell.' Affected by her errant thoughts, her voice came out huskily, and she coughed to clear her throat.

'Our genealogist, of course. Have you changed your mind about doing the interview?'

'Yes, I have. I'm still terrified, but I'll do my best,' Gaelle said.

'That's all we ask. Scott will be delighted, I'm sure.'

Helen went on to discuss the kind of questions they would ask on the air. To her relief, Gaelle found she could answer them easily and naturally. If only she didn't panic at the actual interview, everything would be all right.

'You're going to be fine,' Helen told her after a while. They agreed that the interview would take place the next day, and Helen named a time. 'We'll send a car for you before-hand she said, and hung up.

When the car arrived, Gaelle was ready, although dark-eyed with fatigue and anxiety. She hadn't slept at all the previous night, although her worries had centured more on her own problems than the interview.

At the radio station, she was treated like royalty and shown to a comfortable waiting-room with one glass wall through which she could see Scott Lawson at work. A red 'on air' sign flashed above the entrance to his studio. Helen Otford brought her some coffee, then perched on the edge of the table beside her. 'All you all right?' she queried.

'Apart from feeling as if I'm going to my execution, I'm fine,' said Gaelle with a laugh. 'Will I have long to wait?'

'Not even long enough for a hearty meal,' Helen said. 'You're next, then there's a half-hour newscast, so you needn't hurry out of the studio.'

While a short news bulletin was being broadcast, Gaelle was shown into the studio and settled at a table across from Scott Lawson. A twin of his microphone sat in front of her, and a matching pair of headphones was placed over her ears. Scott Lawson's voice reached her through them. 'Can you hear me OK?'

She nodded, then saw the technician frowning. 'Yes, I can.' The man adjusted some dials and gave Scott a thumbs-up sign.

'We were just getting a level on your voice,' he explained. Seeing the tension in every line of Gaelle's body, he added, 'Just talk to me with the same enthusiasm you did at Megalong and you'll be terrific.'

The mention of Megalong reminded Gaelle why she was here. Scott Lawson was the one person who could lead her to Pete. She relaxed slightly. She needed Pete. She wanted him, a small voice added. This was a small price to pay.

Somehow, the thought got her through the ordeal. Scott Lawson was a skilled interviewer who knew how to draw his guests out on their favourite subject. Under his spell, Gaelle mastered her nerves and answered his questions about family history thoughtfully and well. She even surprised herself by adding some humour, and Scott looked approving.

When the producer finally signalled the end of the programme, Scott helped her to remove the headphones. 'That was marvellous! You really know your stuff.'

'I'm glad you found it interesting,' smiled Gaelle.

'I did, and so did our listeners. Did you see the

switchboard once we invited calls on the open line? It lit up like a Christmas tree!'

'Lots of people are interested in their family's history,' she told him. 'I'm lucky that my field has become trendy.'

'But you also have a knack of putting your knowledge across in an interesting way. It's rarer than you think. Would you come back again? I'm sure we'll get lots of requests.'

Thinking of the strain this interview had cost her, Gaelle laughed nervously. 'I almost had a breakdown coming here! I couldn't do it again.'

Scott glanced at his watch. 'I still have some time. Join me for coffee in my office and I'll try to persuade you to change your mind.'

After praying that she would have a few minutes alone with him after the show, she could hardly believe it was this easy. 'I'd like that,' she agreed.

In his office, she sipped her coffee, waiting for an opening. At last he provided one. 'I'm glad we met at that fund-raiser. For someone who was scared out of her wits, you gave a darned good interview.'

'I'm glad too, now it's over,' she admitted. 'It was a shame you had to leave Megalong early, though. You didn't have much of a break.'

'It's the name of the game,' he said philosophically. 'When something breaks up here, I have to rush back and cover it for the show. It's hardest on my wife and family. They're used to having their plans disrupted, but I hate doing it to them.'

'I understand. I suppose because you were called away Dan had to leave with you.'

The announcer's eyes narrowed as he appraised

her over the rim of his coffee-cup. 'I'm not sure who you mean,' he said carefully.

'Your friend Dan, whom you introduced to Krys when you arrived.'

Scott relaxed slightly. 'Oh Dan—of course! I've been so busy, I almost forgot that he decided to tag along at the last minute.'

Remembering Pete/Dan's assertion that if he had known the theme of the weekend, he wouldn't have come, Gaelle couldn't see how he could have 'tagged along'. But she didn't want to antagonise Scott, so she reverted to the excuse she'd given Krys. 'I took home somthing of his by mistake and I'd like to return it. I lost the paper he gave me with his address, so I was hoping you'd give it to me again.'

'If you give me whatever it is, I'll see that he gets it,' said Scott, outwitting her.

'I'd rather give it to him personally,' she persisted. 'He and I became rather good friends during the weekend.'

'Then it was a shame you didn't guard his address more carefully, isn't it?'

She had the unhappy feeling she wasn't going to get any further with the interviewer. He was used to matching wits with some of the wiliest people in the country, so no amount of subterfuge was going to work. She decided to try the direct approach. 'Scott, I did you a favour by coming on your programme, now I want you to do me one. I need to get in touch with Dan. Believe me, it's vitally important or I wouldn't ask.'

It was the wrong thing to say, she realised as soon as she saw his face darken with annoyance. 'The amount of work you get after being on this show will more than repay any favour you've done me,' he said coolly.

'I'm sorry, I didn't mean it the way it sounded,' she said desperately. This wasn't going the way she had planned at all. 'I must get in touch with Dan.'

'Then leave a message with me. I'll relay it to him.'

She hung her head. 'I can't do that.'

Scott was about to add something more when Helen Otford interrupted them. 'The Prime Minister is arriving downstairs, Scott. Are you ready for him?'

Scott stood up. 'I'll be right down.' With a feeling of despair, Gaelle watched him go. At the door, he turned, all charm and grace again. 'Thanks for the interview, Miss Maxwell. My researcher will show you out and arrange a car to take you home.'

When he had gone, Helen joined her in the office. 'That wasn't so bad, was it? I hear you were a big success.'

But not at what she had come for, Gaelle acknowledged miserably. She hadn't expected Scott to brush off her request so totally. Who on earth was Pete?—Dan, she amended her thought—for she was now convinced they were one and the same. Scott seemed determined to shield him from public view. Added to the false name Dan had given her, she began to wonder what sort of man she had got herself involved with.

Her mind racing, she took her time finishing her coffee while Helen chatted on amiably. Gaelle barely heard what was said, but managed to give non-committal replies. When she could delay her departure no longer, she stood up, an idea forming in her mind.

'Ready to go? ' Helen asked brightly.

'Yes, I just need the file of background material I brought for Scott.'

Gaelle reached across the desk and tugged at her folder, making sure she brought a wave of paper cascading off the desk with it, then pretending alarm. 'Oh, look what I've done!—I'm sorry.' She dropped to her knees and began scooping up the papers.

'It's all right, I'll pick them up later,' said Helen, sounding strained.

'It was my clumsiness. I insist.'

Among the fallen papers was an executive diary she'd seen Scott consulting when he sat at the desk. Adding it to the pile in her arms, she flipped it open casually. As she'd hoped, his name and address were in the panel headed, 'If lost, please return to . . .' Even celebrities could be naïve sometimes, thank goodness.

Quickly she fixed the address in her mind, then replaced the pile of papers on the desk. 'I'm sorry—I must be on edge.'

'It's quite all right.' All the same, the researcher seemed relieved to be able to escort Gaelle out of the office and down to the lobby where a car was called for her. On the way, Gaelle passed Scott deep in conversation with a man she recognised as the Prime Minister, followed by an entourage of security men. None of them paid her any attention.

Once in the car and on her way home, she scribbled Scott's address on the back of a file before it could slip her mind. If she couldn't persuade him to put her in touch with Dan at the studio, maybe she'd have better luck in the relaxed atmosphere of his home.

She waited until early evening to go to the address she'd memorised, hoping Scott would have had time to unwind after his programme, making him more approachable than he had been this morning. She hadn't a clue what to say if he asked her how she obtained his address, but she decided to cross that bridge when she reached it. For now, she was only concerned with how to convince him that she simply must see Dan again.

Was it only the baby which was making her so determined to see him? she asked herself as she drove. She had to admit she wanted to see him for herself as well. After telling herself she was better off to forget him, it wasn't so easy in practice. In a brief encounter, Pete had made a devastating impact on her, more than any man she had ever known.

Scott's house was in a bayside suburb. She had some difficulty locating it, but found it at last by counting down from its neighbours. Hidden behind a jungle wall of monstera deliciosa and flowering hibiscus shrubs, it was a peach-coloured, oddly angled house with a flat roof. Leaving her car parked in the street outside, Gaelle approached the house cautiously, half-expecting fences, alarms and guard dogs to bar her way.

But there were no dogs and, seemingly, no alarms. She reached the front door unchallenged. Still feeling some trepidation, she pressed the doorbell and heard it reverberate deep inside the house.

It felt like an age before she heard footsteps and saw the shadowy outline of a man through the frosted-glass panes of the door. She wiped her moist palms against her dress. Scott had to listen to her this time, he had to!

'There's no need to ring, I don't have a blonde in here,' he said as he opened the door.

Then they both froze, he with apparent surprise and she with shock. He must have expected to see Scott standing there. And whoever she had steeled herself to meet, it wasn't the tall, broad-shouldered man facing her now.

'Pete!' she breathed in astonishment. 'I mean Dan.'

He recovered first. 'What the hell are you doing here?'

CHAPTER FOUR

GAELLE examined the granite planes of Pete's face, and finally forced her eyes to meet his searching green ones, but could find no sign of warmth or welcome. She said the first thing that came into her head. 'I'm looking for you.'

His expression remained unforgiving. 'Well, you've found me. What do you want?'

Whatever response she had imagined, it wasn't this attitude of complete dismissal. She couldn't believe she had misread his feelings for her so totally. When they had made love at Megalong, Pete had felt something for her, she could swear to it. Now he was acting as if she had been a night's diversion and no more. Could she have been so wrong about him? Coldness crept over her. But she couldn't just turn and walk away as no doubt he would like her to. 'We need to talk,' she insisted.

He hesitated, then grabbed her by the arm and hustled her indoors. Bewildered, Gaelle watched him inspect the garden before he closed the door and slammed home a security bolt. 'What are you expecting—my big brother?' she asked. 'I came here by myself.'

He swung his gaze to her and she felt the chill of it. 'So I see. You wanted to talk, so go ahead.'

They were standing in a vast entrance hall

47

decorated with navy suede wallpaper and gleaming white woodwork. The only homelike touch was a tall brass urn filled with pampas-grass. She couldn't bring herself to blurt out her news in such an impersonal setting. 'Can't we sit down somewhere?' she asked.

Pete's mouth twisted into a sneer. 'The setting shouldn't matter—if you really came here to talk.'

Perplexed, she stared at him. 'What else could I be after?'

'You'd be surprised.'

'What's that supposed to mean?'

He seemed about to answer, then thought better of it. Instead, he raked a hand through his thick hair, spiking it. 'Oh, for goodness' sake, come in then,' he snapped.

Gaelle followed him into the most unusual living-room she'd ever seen. It was like something out of *House and Garden*. More suede covered the walls, this time in a rich rust colour. A high-peaked timber ceiling was accented with black beams, drawing the eyes upwards to a library level accessible by a set of movable steps. Gaelle thought she recognised the unusual rust, black and white fabric covering the furniture as the work of a famous designer. A bar covered in the same material filled a deep bay window which overlooked the tree-studded garden. A pool sparkled among the trees. 'This is fabulous!' she exclaimed.

'Yes, isn't it?'

Pete's dry tone reminded her that this wasn't a social call. She took the seat he indicated, perching gingerly on the edge to avoid being swallowed up by the deep upholstery. The tense pose added to her uneasiness.

He sat down opposite her, his long legs more easily coping with the cushioning. He looked as if he could leap to his feet without effort. Gaelle swallowed hard. 'I didn't expect to find you here,' she began.

He arched one eyebrow in cynical disbelief, 'Oh, no? What are you then, an Avon lady who got lucky?'

Anger made her bristle. 'You don't have to be rude! Of course it wasn't luck. I was hoping to find Scott Lawson at home.'

'Are you and Scott seeing each other?'

Did she imagine it, or was there the faintest hint of jealousy in his tone? 'I know Scott,' she said carefully, watching his reaction.

She was in for a disappointment. 'If you know Scott, then you know he isn't living here at the moment. He's staying at his penthouse in the city so I can use the house. But you didn't know that, did you?'

Unhappily, she shook her head. 'It's true, I came to see Scott. But I wanted him to help me locate you.'

'So you didn't expect to find me here?'

'No. How could I?'

Some of the tension went out of him and he relaxed for the first time since she had arrived. 'I can't tell you how glad I am to hear you say that,' he murmured.

'What did you think I was—a spy?' She regretted the outburst as soon as his expression grew thunderous. 'Look, I don't know who you are or what's going on here, but the reason I need to see you is entirely personal, I swear. Do you believe me?'

'God knows, I shouldn't after the warnings I've

had, but yes, I believe you.'

'Warnings?' she blurted out. 'What kind of warnings?'

'Nothing you should concern yourself about,' he assured her. 'What did you come here to discuss?'

Now that the moment was there, Gaelle found she couldn't come right out and say she was pregnant with his child. It seemed so cold and unfeeling. 'Would you mind if I had a drink first? This is kind of difficult,' she said.

He shrugged, as if it didn't matter to him either way, but he strode over to the bar and opened a refrigerator at the back of it. 'White wine?' he offered. 'There's a very nice Chablis on ice here.'

'Fine, thanks,' she said distractedly. It didn't matter what she drank, as long as she could put off the moment of truth. Suddenly she had another thought. 'You still haven't told me your real name.'

He paused in the act of pouring their drinks. Absently she noticed that he drank neat whisky. 'Does it matter?' he asked.

'It does to me. I told you mine.'

He placed her drink on a coffee table in front of her, then sat down, nursing his own. 'And I lied to you about who I was, as you obviously know. I'm sorry about that. My real name is Dan Buckhorn.'

Dan Buckhorn. Gaelle let the name echo around her mind, savouring its ruggedly masculine sound. Then she asked, 'Why did you lie?'

He drained his glass and set it down. 'I had my reasons.'

Reasons which he didn't intend to share with her, she thought, her anger flaring. 'Is this a game with you?' she demanded.

'You were all playing a game that weekend,' he reminded her. 'I only went along.'

'But only because it suited you. You said yourself that you weren't involved in the murder mystery.'

'I had enough mysteries of my own.' Something softened suddenly in the mineral-green eyes, and he rubbed them, as if to drive the weakness away. 'Look, Gaelle, I'm sorry about what happened at Megalong. I didn't want to deceive you, but I didn't have a choice. It's better if you don't know all the details, for your own sake.'

'And I'm expected to be happy with that explanation?' Which wasn't any explanation at all, she thought.

'No, not happy. But I hope you'll accept it for now.'

There was something touchingly earnest in the way he looked at her, his eyes imploring her to trust him. A shiver rippled down her spine, and she took a sip of wine to rid herself of the feeling that someone had just walked over her grave. 'Very well, I guess it isn't the most important thing,' she agreed.

Dan seem genuinely relieved. 'Thank you.'

'There is one thing I need to know,' she added, and saw him tense again.

'Yes?'

'Are you sorry that we made love?'

'God, no!' His explosive response carried all the conviction she needed to know that he was telling the truth. He wasn't indifferent to her, after all.

'I'm glad. When you were so cold to me just now, I thought it had all been on my side.'

He leaned back in his chair, his eyes coming alive with interest as the coolness seeped out of them. 'I don't suppose you'd go away even if I said you were a one-night stand?'

'No. I wouldn't, because I know it isn't true.'

His gaze became reluctantly admiring. 'You don't give up easily, do you, Gaelle Maxwell?'

'If I did, I wouldn't be the sort of woman to interest you,' she said, astonished at her brazenness. She had never spoken to a man like that before. But she felt driven to make Dan understand the importance of their meeting to her.

'You're right,' he conceded. 'I knew going to bed with you at Megalong was a mistake.' Before she could frame an angry retort, he added, 'Too bad I couldn't stop myself from making it.'

'Me, neither,' she confessed.

He stood up and towered over her, then took her arms and urged her to her feet until she was standing a heartbeat away from him. He was wearing the same citrus aftershave lotion she remembered from Megalong, and its heady scent invaded her nostrils. It had an odd effect on her breathing too, because it was suddenly an effort to pull air into her lungs. 'Dan?' she said softly.

He bent his head towards her. 'I think I'm about to make another mistake,' he muttered.

Since the weekend at Megalong, she had dreamed of being in his arms again, but her imagination was no match for the reality. There was no way she could imagine the way her heart beat faster or her pulses raced, nor the way the blood sang in her veins. Nor could she conjure up the sense of flying through space and time, as his mouth commanded hers to respond. No fantasy could compare with the reality of his arms around her as his body pressed close against hers, awakening them both to feverish arousal.

Distantly, Gaelle remembered why she was here and she began to struggle free. Dan released her but regarded her curiously. 'What's the matter?' he asked.

'You,' she said, mastering her voice with an effort. 'This wasn't why I came here.'

'Pity,' he said. 'I was just starting to remember why I was so attracted to you at Megalong.'

'Stop it! Sex isn't the be-all and end-all of a relationship,' she snapped, annoyed that she had allowed herself to get so carried away. She hadn't intended it to happen, any more than she had intended it at Megalong. But Dan could inflame her in a way no man had ever done before.

She was about to resume her seat, then thought better of it. As long as they were in the same room, she couldn't trust herself not to end up in his arms again. 'Can we go for a walk?' she asked.

'Only around the house,' said Dan, his tone sharp. Then he added, more kindly, 'This place has magnificent grounds and they're very private. Would you like to see them?'

Privacy was the last thing she wanted right now, but Dan seemed to need it, so she nodded. 'All right.'

She was disturbingly conscious of his hand on her arm as he led her through a dining-room decorated as lavishly as the living-room, then to a sunroom which had tall windows on three sides, letting sunlight stream in. The room opened on to a vast, covered deck and the pool she had glimpsed from the living-room.

Tall palm trees ringed the pool, then the land was terraced until it dropped away to the Harbour far below. The side boundaries were marked by hedges of bamboo that screened the property from its neighbours. More flowering hibiscus shrubs dotted the lawn, so the effect was one of tropical lushness and inviting coolness. 'It's lovely out here,' breathed Gaelle, bending down to stroke a huge black and white cat that lolled on the stone-flagged path.

'That's Jenkins, Scott's cat,' Dan explained. 'He's good company—quiet and undemanding.'

She looked up at him. 'Is that a hint?'

Out in the garden, he seemed more relaxed, more human, she thought, surprised. Perhaps the outdoors suited him better. 'Are you the outdoor type?' she asked.

'Definitely. Being shut inside makes me feel like a caged animal.'

The savagery in his tone startled her. 'Then why must you put up with it?'

'Right now, I have no choice. But we didn't come out here to talk about me.' He led her to a wrought-iron and slatted timber bench nestled among the bushes, and guided her on to it. 'No more delaying tactics. What did you want to se me about?'

Had she been delaying the moment? Yes, she accepted. As long as they strolled together through the grounds, she could pretend they were lovers, here by choice. Once she told Dan her news, their futures became bound together in a way he might not like. But he was as much to blame as she was, she reminded herself. She took a deep breath. 'I think I'm pregnant,' she said as calmly as she could.

He watched her for a moment, unblinking, then he stood up and gazed out to sea. 'What makes you think it's mine?'

'You bastard!' Of all the reactions she'd imagined, this wasn't one of them. Anger and humiliation brought her to her feet, her fists pounding against his back until he swung around and caught her flailing hands.

'That's enough!' he gritted.

'Well, you apologise for that crack!' she shouted. 'You're the only man who could possibly be the father.'

'All right, I take it back. But I wasn't to know, was I?'

She struggled in his grip. 'I'm telling you, it's the truth. Let me go!'

'When you promise to talk about this calmly.'

'It's difficult when you're accused of being a . . . a . . .' She spluttered on a word which would fit the behaviour he'd accused her of.

'I said I'm sorry,' he repeated. 'Now, will you be calm?'

Exhausted from fighting him, Gaelle slumped in his grasp. 'All right, I'll try.'

'Good girl!' He eased his grip on her hands and she sank back on to the bench, rubbing her wrists and watching him warily.

'Now, don't eat me,' he cautioned, 'but if it's money you need . . .'

'I didn't come to extort money from you,' she

seethed, half rising to attack him again. 'My baby needs a father.'

Dan forestalled her, pushing her gently but firmly back down again. 'I see. So you want me to marry you.'

'No!' She hadn't considered such a thing. 'I only want your assurance that you'll be available when my baby needs you. I don't want him growing up not knowing who his father is or what he looks like. Is it too much to ask?'

His expression had softened, and she was startled by the vulnerability she saw there. 'Dan,' she said gently, 'did you hear what I said?'

His voice came to her from a great distance. 'I heard you, and you're right. No child should grow up without knowing its parents. I would never do that to any child of mine.'

There was such pain in his words that she flinched. 'Dan, what's the matter?'

She cried out in alarm as he gripped her upper arms so tightly that she felt the bruising start. Half pulling her out of the seat, he bent his face to hers. 'If this baby means anything to you, marry me,' he said.

'I can't,' she gasped, tears of pain and shock pricking her eyes. 'I didn't come here to blackmail you into a proposal, honestly.'

He eased her grip a little, but did not release her. 'You don't have to blackmail me, I'm ready and willing.'

'How can I marry you when I hardly know you?' she cried wildly. 'All we had was one night of love.'

'We could have more,' Dan vowed. 'We're meant for each other, you know that as well as I do.'

'You didn't know it until I said I was pregnant,' she said shakily. 'Until then, you couldn't wait for me to get out of your life.'

'This is different. We could be a family.'

'Not if all I am to you is a brood mare!' she retorted.

Shock darkened his features and he seemed to return to his senses. He set her down carefully. 'I'm sorry, Gaelle—I didn't mean to suggest any such thing. I guess your news shook me up so I went a little crazy. Forgive me?'

His smile was so appealing that her heart did a somersault in response. 'I suppose I should be pleased that you're so happy,' she conceded. 'Not every man would be thrilled with the news.'

'How did it happen?' he asked unexpectedly.

She was tempted to be flippant, then saw that he was really concerned for her. 'There was a man in my life, Nick Guardino,' she explained. 'We were unofficially engaged for two years. But the longer we were together, the more I understood what I'd be getting into if I married him. He believed in the old "barefoot and pregnant" axiom to the point of absurdity. He hated me having a career, and made it clear that I would have to give it up to be his wife.'

'So you gave him up,' Dan observed.

'It wasn't easy. We were together for a long time. Apart from his old-fashioned attitudes, he's a wonderful man, considerate and charming. But he has to be the boss, while I happen to think marriage should be a partnership.'

Dan looked thoughtful. 'Yet you gave to me what you'd kept from him all that time.'

Gaelle coloured at the memory. Dan couldn't help

but know that she had never given herself to Nick. She'd started taking the pill when they had begun to discuss marriage. But when Nick had found out, he'd read the riot act to her, as if she was immoral for even taking it. 'That was the beginning of the end of our relationship,' she told Dan. 'I was so upset at Nick's reaction that I stopped taking anything.'

'And then I came along,' said Dan, warming her with his gentle tone. 'I'm sorry, Gaelle.'

'Please don't be sorry,' she implored. 'I was an only child and my parents couldn't have any more, so I grew up longing for younger brothers and sisters. Then I looked forward to having my own family. I didn't think it would happen like this, but I'm not sorry.'

'Well, that's something, at least.'

'Did you have any brothers or sisters?' she asked.

He shook his head. 'There's only Scott. He's my foster-brother.'

Dan's family must have been taken Scott in when he was younger, she realised. 'Maybe that's what my parents should have done, fostered a child,' she said. 'By the time they realised they couldn't have any more, they were too old to adopt.'

'Yes,' he said shortly. 'We'd better go inside, it's getting cool. I don't want you catching a cold in your condition.'

He sounded so anxious that Gaelle had to hold back a smile. 'I should tell you my doctor hasn't confirmed I'm pregnant,' she explained. 'She was fairly sure, but I have to wait for the results.'

'What do you think the answer is?' he asked, taking her arm to help her along the uneven path.

'I'm sure.' And she was. Ever since she'd seen Jill, she had known in her heart of hearts that she was expecting a child. Her body felt different, somehow, although there were no physical changes as yet to explain it. But she knew.

Dan nodded, accepting the mystical process as a fact. 'In that case, so am I.'

It was early evening and the shadows were lengthening around the garden, so she had to watch her step on the flagstones. Suddenly a sharp pain knifed through her and she stumbled. Only Dan's hand on her arm kept her from falling. 'Careful,' he warned her. 'This path is slippery.'

But it wasn't the path. With growing horror, she felt the pain come again, and almost doubled over with the strength of it. Her breath came in laboured gasps as she fought for control. Then it came again, and she felt something warm and moist trickle down her legs.

'Gaelle, what is it?' Dan asked, fear in his voice.

'Call my doctor, quickly,' she implored. 'Something's wrong. I think it's the baby!'

CHAPTER FIVE

WITHOUT another word, Dan swept Gaelle into his arms and carried her inside. When she was settled on the couch, he riffled through her bag and found her address book. Through a haze of pain and fear she heard him telephone Jill, his voice low and urgent.

'Luckily she was in her surgery. She'll be here in half an hour,' he told her.

'I hope she hurries,' Gaelle gasped out. 'I don't want to lose the baby!'

She felt herself slipping into a fog of pain, and wasn't sure what he said next. It sounded like, 'There'll be other babies. Just as long as you're all right.' But she must have imagined that part. He hadn't wanted to see her until she'd mentioned the child. She must have it the wrong way around.

Something damp and cool was placed on her burning forehead, then Dan pulled a chair up to the couch and slipped his hands into hers. 'The doctor won't be long,' he told her.

She smiled weakly. 'Jill's a good friend.'

'Have you known her long?'

Even while she recognised that he wanted to keep her from thinking too much, she was grateful. He must care. 'We met at evening college,' she explained. 'We were in the same craft class.'

'You go in for this craft stuff in a big way, don't

you?'

She nodded, and wished she hadn't when a wave of pain assailed her. Dan's grip on her hand tightened. 'My grandmother taught me to make shuttle lace—or tatting, as she called it. It's restful and productive at the same time.'

'Sssh, try to relax,' he instructed as she drew another sharp breath.

Gaelle shook her head. 'Talking helps. Do you have any hobbies?'

'One, but it's neither restful nor productive. I jump out of aeroplanes.'

Her eyes widened. 'Parachuting?'

'Mmm-hmm.'

'But isn't it dangerous?'

'Maybe that's why I like it, although my friends say it's a busman's holiday.'

'Your work is dangerous too? What do you do?' she asked.

He smoothed out the compress on her forehead. 'I think you should get some rest.'

Before she could protest, Dan had gone to the window, presumably looking for Jill's car. 'She's here,' he said over his shoulder. 'I'll let her in.'

Then Jill was at her side, clucking over her as she conducted her examination. Dan left them alone, saying he would make some tea.

Gaelle regarded Jill fearfully. 'The baby's gone, isn't it?'

Jill sighed. 'Women always know these things instinctively. Yes, I'm afraid you miscarried.'

'But why? What happened?'

'No one knows. Nature has a way of making sure

that only healthy pregnancies go ahead at this stage.'

'You mean there was something wrong with the baby?'

'Either that, or you weren't ready to have it yet. It was early days for you to be fertile again.'

'So that's the end of that.' Gaelle's brave words were instantly contradicted by the tears that welled in her eyes and spilled down her cheeks. She wiped at them angrily. 'What's the matter with me?' she muttered.

'You've had a shock, both physically and mentally,' Jill told her gently. 'You'll need rest and time to get over it. I could send you to hospital for a few days.'

'I'd rather go home, please.'

'I'd prefer you to be with someone, at least for a day or so. Is there anyone you can stay with?'

'She can stay here,' said a voice from the doorway.

Jill looked relieved. 'It's settled, then. I'd rather you didn't get up for twenty-four hours. With Dan to take care of you . . .'

'I couldn't impose on him,' Gaelle interrupted. Jill was acting as if Dan was an old friend! 'I'll be fine at home.'

'In that case, hospital might be best.'

Gaelle wavered. It seemed she had a choice between going to hospital or staying here. She didn't want to be hospitalised, and yet she balked at staying here with Dan now that the only reason he wanted her around was gone. But it seemed as if she had no choice. 'Very well, I'll stay,' she said resignedly.

Jill gave her a curious look, and Gaelle wondered

how much Dan had told her about their true relationship. I'm so glad. If you stay in bed for today and tomorrow, you should be fine. I'll check on you late tomorrow just to make sure everything's all right.'

'Don't worry, I'll take care of her,' Dan assured Jill. The doctor walked him over to the window and Gaelle heard them conferring in lowered tones. They were talking about her, she gathered, but she felt too tired and depressed to object. Knowing Jill, she was probably briefing Dan on the care of the patient. Jill did fuss so! It was only a little problem.

Only a little problem. Was that all her baby would ever be? Misery overwhelmed her and she gave in to the tears banked up behind her eyes. She muffled her sobs in a cushion to avoid alerting Jill and Dan. She had just been getting used to the idea that she was pregnant, had even begun to make plans for herself and the baby. Now there was nothing to plan for.

She tried to tell herself that the baby had been only a speck of tissue, not really a person at all. It didn't stem her tears. But were they all for the baby? Shocked, she faced the fact that some of her tears were for herself. She was the mother of his child, so Dan had wanted to marry her. Absurd though it was, she found the idea curiously thrilling. But he hadn't wanted to see her again until she told him about the baby. Now he had no more reason to want her around.

'Are you asleep?' Jill asked softly, startling her.

Gaelle turned her head. 'No, I was just thinking.'

Wisely, Jill ignored her wet cheeks and shining

eyes. 'Well, don't think too much. Talk to Dan about it. He'll understand. Don't bottle your feelings up, OK?'

Mustering a smile, Gaelle nodded. 'You're the doctor.'

'Remember it,' said Jill with mock severity. She picked up her bag. 'I have to go now—I'm on call at the hospital. I've told Dan what to do for you, and I'll call back tomorrow.'

Gaelle returned her handclasp. 'Thanks for everything, Jill. 'I'm glad you were here.'

Dan showed the doctor out, then returned with two cups of steaming tea. He placed one on the low table beside Gaelle's couch, and she frowned. 'You don't have to wait on me. I don't want to be a nuisance.'

'You're not a nuisance,' he insisted. 'Remember, I'm partly responsible for what happened to you.'

So that was why he'd agreed to let her stay, she thought grimly. He felt guilty about his part in this. At the same time, she recalled how insistent he had been to marry her and provide the baby with a father. He must be feeling the loss as keenly as she was. 'I'm sorry about the baby,' she said.

'I am too. Now it's over, I realise how much I liked the idea of being a father.' He stared into space, his expression thoughtful.

Being a father, but not a husband, she noted. Maybe it was for the best. Dan might have wanted the child, but he didn't want a wife; he had made that clear when she'd turned up on his doorstep today. If she had come on her own behalf, she was sure he would have sent her away.

She drank her tea, grateful for its soothing warmth. 'Won't Scott Lawson mind me staying here?' she queried. 'It is his house.'

'Actually, it belongs to me,' he told her. 'Scott uses it when I'm overseas or interstate, which saves it standing empty for long periods. But his real home is his city penthouse. So it's up to me who stays here.'

'Lucky for me,' she said sleepily. Whatever Jill had given her was making her drowsy. 'Why did Scott have this address in his notebook?'

'So that's how you found the place. Quite the detective, aren't you?'

'Research is my stock-in-trade, remember?' she reminded him.

'Ah, yes, the genealogist. Scott does most of his entertaining here because it's roomier than his place, which is why he carries the address with him. But he should be more careful.'

It was an effort to keep her eyes open. 'Why?' she asked.

'Some weirdos get their kicks out of harassing famous people,' he observed. 'And occasionally the not-so-famous.'

'Are you famous?'

'Infamous,' he said shortly, and stood up. 'I'd better get you to bed.'

'Please, I'm a sick woman!'

'You're also high on Jill's potions, so don't make offers you can't deliver on,' he said with a laugh.

This happy, floaty feeling must be due to Jill's medication, Gaelle realised. Somewhere deep inside her, depression still lurked. But for now, she could push it away and rest, as Jill must have intended. She hardly felt Dan lift her up and carry her to a bedroom. 'Sleep tight,' he said. 'The bathroom's just next door and has everything you could need.' Then his lips brushed her forehead and she knew no more.

It was dark when she awoke, disturbed by the sound of men's voices coming from the living-room. As she struggled to full wakefulness, she realised she was wearing an oversized T-shirt and nothing else. Dan must have put it on her when he'd put her to bed, but she had no memory of it. She squinted at a clock built into the bedhead. It was almost midnight. She had slept for hours.

Dimly she recalled Dan saying something about a bathroom next door, and she headed for it, hoping she wouldn't meet anyone on the way. But the conversation didn't falter, so evidently no one had heard her get up.

On the way back to the bedroom, the sound of her own name caught her attention and she recognised Scott Lawson's distinctive tones. 'You can't let her stay here, Dan. You know the risk.'

Then came Dan's calm voice. 'Relax! She didn't even know I was here. She came looking for you, hoping you'd help her to find me.'

'Geez, Dan, first she snoops around the studio, then she tracks you here and stays on some pretext—she could be the one you're worried about.'

'You're the one who's worried, not me. But it was no pretext, believe me. Gaelle isn't one of them, so put your mind at rest.'

'How can I, when at any moment . . .'

'Keep your voice down, will you?'

At Dan's sharp command, the voices dropped and

Gaelle could make out no more of what they were saying. Puzzled, she returned to her room. What was going on here, and who did Scott Lawson fear she was?

CHAPTER SIX

WHEN next Gaelle awoke, sunlight was streaming into the room. She smiled as she remembered over-hearing Scott's comments last night. In daylight, they seemed so melodramatic that she must have dreamed them.

The smile was still on her lips when Dan walked in. He carried a tray and looked approving when he saw her expression. 'I'm glad you're feeling better this morning,' he said.

'Much better,' she agreed. 'Whatever Jill gave me, I slept like a baby.' Her voice caught as she used the expression, and sadness flickered across her face. 'I didn't mean . . .'

'It's all right,' he cut in. 'You can't excise the word "baby" from the language. Jill said it was better if you talked about it, remember?'

'I know. I just didn't realise I'd feel so badly about it. It hardly existed, after all.'

'It was real to both of us,' he said firmly. He placed the tray across her knees and helped her to sit up. 'You'll feel better once you've eaten something.'

He had prepared a plate of fluffy scrambled eggs and golden toast to tempt her. Gaelle sniffed at the single rose set on one side of the tray. 'You're very kind,' she smiled.

'Not kind—worried about you. I want you to get

well.'

Well away from here? she wondered, thinking about the conversation she'd overheard last night. She was still not sure whether she'd dreamed it or not. She started to ask him about it when he forestalled her by wheeling a television set to the foot of the bed. 'I've brought you a pile of magazines and the TV,' he said. 'I'd like to sit with you, but I have to work.'

She masked her disappointment. 'I understand. What are you doing?'

'Working up a new computer programme,' Dan explained. He opened the french doors leading to the garden and pointed to a low building across the pool from her. 'I use the *cabaña* as an office, so I'll be within earshot. If you need anything, just call.'

'Thanks, but you seem to have thought of everything.'

He nodded, then leaned across and brushed her forehead with his lips. It was the kind of kiss any two acquaintances might exchange, but it set Gaelle's senses tingling. She was immediately conscious of the skimpy T-shirt and the fact that she had nothing on underneath it. But Dan paid no heed to her blushing response as he stepped out of the french doors and strode around the pool and towards the *cabaña*. Moments later she heard the clack-clack of a keyboard as he went to work.

Pensively, she began to eat her breakfast. He had said his work was dangerous, but computer programming wasn't dangerous, surely? Unless he was working on something top secret that criminals wanted to steal. She shook herself mentally. Being around him was fostering a cloak-and-dagger mentality. She'd have to stop it or she'd be seeing danger around every corner, like Dan.

The flicker of a shadow across her window made her start, until she realised it was only Jenkins, come to visit her. The cat climbed on to the bed and settled across her legs with a contented purr. Gaelle stroked it and smiled. 'For a minute there, I thought you were a spy!' she told the animal.

All the same, as she watched the morning programmes and leafed through the magazines Dan had brought, her gaze kept going to the window. What she expected to see, she couldn't say, but she felt uneasy. There were no more shadows across the window, only the occasional snap of a twig in the front garden, and she told herself it was probably another cat. She made herself concentrate on the television.

Dan joined her for lunch, then Jill arrived to check on her patient. 'I think it's safe for you to go home now,' she told Gaelle.

When she had gone, Dan returned looking happy. 'Aren't you pleased with Jill's news?' he asked her.

She should have been, but the thought of returning to her empty house witout Dan was oddly disquieting. She was careful not to let him see what she was thinking. 'Of course I'm pleased. I'll be able to get on with my work again—I have a family tree to finish for a client this week.'

'Hey, I thought Jill told you to rest,' he reminded her.

'I won't overdo it,' she promised him, nevertheless pleased by his concern. She threw back the covers—

then wished she'd waited. She'd forgotten how skimpy the borrowed T-shirt was, until she saw his gaze linger on her long, nut-brown legs, then travel slowly upwards. 'God, Gaelle,' he said huskily, 'you could stay, you know.'

Her heartbeat picked up pace as she thought of what his comment might mean. Unless he was hoping for another baby from her? 'I can't, Dan,' she said flatly, chilled by the thought.

His face cleared abruptly. 'What am I thinking about? Of course you can't. I'll drive you home.'

'But my car is parked outside,' she reminded him, stung by the change in his attitude. He sounded anxious to be rid of her again.

His next words confirmed it. 'Then I'll drive you home in your car and catch a taxi back.'

Gaelle didn't feel up to driving herself and, crazily, she ached for a few extra minutes in his company. 'Very well,' she agreed. 'Just let me get showered and dressed.'

They accomplished the drive to her terrace house in Clontarf in strained silence, like two strangers who didn't know what to say to each other. Which was fairly accurate, she thought miserably. For all that had passed between them, they were still virtual strangers. All the same, she felt the urge to keep Dan with her for just a little longer. 'Won't you come inside for coffee?' she asked as he parked her car outside her house.

'I'd better not, you need to rest.' He looked up and down the street before getting out of the car and opening her door. 'I'll see you to your front door.'

So that was that, she thought miserably. She felt a

terrible sense of loss as he left her at her door and strode off down the street towards the taxi stand she'd pointed out to him. Several cars waited there, so he would have no trouble hailing one. She'd been hoping he would say something about seeing her again, but he hadn't, and now it was too late. Soon he would be gone.

She watched as he reached the corner, only then remembering that she still had his T-shirt with her. She'd packed it in her shopping bag and had forgotten it belonged to him until now. 'Dan, wait!' she called after his retreating figure. Suddenly her voice dropped, almost as if she didn't want him to hear her. 'I have to give you back your T-shirt.'

He didn't react, and she felt a sudden rush of warmth as she realised she had the perfect excuse to see him again. That he had given no sign of wanting to see her, she refused to accept. She would believe it when he told her to her face.

With a feeling of relief, she closed the front door behind her and leaned against it. She would see him again.

Cheered by the thought, she looked around the narrow hallway of her terrace house. It was one of her favourite parts of the house with its yellow-painted front door, black and white chequered floor tiles, and a huge 'Fire Danger' sign bought at an auction, adding a touch of novelty. A splash of yellow on the floor was out of place, and she bent to pick up the telegram she had overlooked.

Her heart turned over as she recognised that the sender was Jill and the message carried yesterday's date. With shaking hands, she smoothed the page out and focused on the words, not wanting to read them, yet knowing that she must. 'Congratulations. Test positive. Call for appointment schedule,' Jill's message said.

Slowly Gaelle tore the sheet into postage-stamp-sized pieces. This time yesterday she had been expecting Dan's child. Now it was gone. Dropping her bag, she hurried into her peppermint-green bedroom and threw herself on to the bed, crying as if she would never stop.

After a long time, the tears ended and she took a leisurely bath to wash away the last of her sorrow. Tomorrow was a new day, and she already knew what she was going to do. She would return Dan's T-shirt and find out once and for all whether they had any future. Until then she busied herself working on her computer, printing out the last of her current project. That done, she packaged it ready to mail to the client on her way to see Dan, then made herself some supper and went to bed early.

Several cars were parked in Dan's street when she pulled up there next morning, so she was forced to leave her car half a block away from his house. As she walked towards it, she hugged the freshly laundered T-shirt to her, hoping he wouldn't see her excuse for what it was, a blatant need to see him again.

She'd spent a large part of last night thinking about him and wondering about the attraction he exerted for her, but fell asleep no closer to reaching a conclusion. Maybe he was right. Maybe there was such a thing as fatal attraction, she thought, remembering her parents' romance.

Distracted by her thoughts, she didn't see the man

until she had her hand on Dan's front gate. Then she froze at the sight of a figure dressed all in black, moving furtively from window to window, as if trying to gain entry to the house. He carried something bulky in one hand, and Gaelle felt sick as she recognised it as a gun.

Hurriedly, she backed away, but not before she'd caught sight of a tall, broad-shouldered figure moving around inside. Dear God! The man must be after Dan. The intruder hadn't seen her, thank goodness, so she sped back the way she'd come, heading for a telephone box on the corner.

With shaking hands she dialled the police emergency number and explained what she'd seen. 'Please hurry!' she urged, as fear for Dan turned her blood to ice.

The police officer instructed her to remain in the booth, out of sight. Gaelle felt hemmed in by the cubicle, but agreed to do as requested. At least she could see Dan's house from here. She tensed as she waited for the sound of a gunshot.

When it came, she almost collapsed with fear for Dan. No longer caring for her own safety, she stumbled out of the box and raced back towards his house, dreading what she might find.

A scream tore from her lungs as she was caught from behind in an irresistible grip. A hand clamped over her mouth, silencing her. 'It's all right, I've got you.'

The scream died in her throat as she recognised Dan's voice. He dragged her into the shelter of some bushes before he uncovered her mouth. She stared at him, wild-eyed. 'Dan, you're all right! But you were in there—I saw you!'

'No, that was a police decoy.'

'You mean they're here already?'

'They've been here for two days, watching the house.'

A giddy sense of unreality overtook her. 'Watching the house? Why? What's happening?'

'Remember I told you that some weirdos get their kicks out of harassing other people?' She nodded. 'This is one of those times.'

'You mean someone's been threatening you?'

'Yes, but not for much longer. Look.'

Unwillingly, Gaelle dragged her gaze away from Dan in time to see a group of burly men in business suits escort the black-clad intruder to a waiting car. Only when he was safely inside and flanked by two of the men did Dan emerge from their hiding-place and walked her towards the house.

One of the men saluted Dan. 'We got him, sir. He won't trouble you any further.'

'Thanks, Detective Barr. I'll sleep a lot easier knowing he's in custody.'

The detective grinned. 'We've got enough on this character to put him away for life! But we'll still need your statement.'

'You'll have it,' Dan assured him. 'I'll be down later to give it to you.'

'Fine, sir. Have a good day.'

'I will now,' Dan agreed. They watched as the detective got into another of the cars which Gaelle realised now were unmarked police cars, and drove away.

'Now will you tell me what this is all about?' she

asked weakly.

Dan led her inside and put a drink into her hands before he answered. 'The man they just arrested is an international terrorist.'

'Why was he after you with a gun?'

'He wanted to kill me,' he said matter-of-factly. She felt her bones turn to jelly.

'Oh, Dan!' A band of pain tightened around her chest at the thought. 'Why would he want to do that?'

He sat down beside her on the couch and pulled her close to him. 'Don't sound so scared! It's all over. He won't be back.'

'But why was he here at all? Who are you, Dan?'

'Nobody, really. I'm a consultant on airport safety. Governments call me in when they want to improve security at major airports.'

Bewildered, Gaelle looked up at him. 'But you said you worked with computers.'

'I said I was programming a computer,' he corrected her. 'International terrorists are becoming increasingly clever at evading our security measures, and the latest trick is to use all-plastic firearms to avoid detection. I'm developing a computer program to counteract the problem.'

'I see,' she said. 'That man was one of the terrorists you're out to stop, so he wanted to get to you first.'

He ruffled her hair affectionately. 'Smart girl! I've been getting threats ever since I came back to Australia, which is why Scott thought it was a good idea to hide me away at Megalong under a false name. Then he suggested I work here, since very few people know I own this house.'

Now she understood Scott's consternation when he found out that she was staying here. He was worried that she was part of a gang stalking Dan. No wonder he hadn't wanted to give her any information about Dan's whereabouts! 'Are you safe now?' she asked worriedly.

His hold on her tightened. 'As safe as one can be in my line of work.'

Gaelle was trembling so violently that she could hardly keep her voice steady. 'When I saw that gunman at your window, with you inside, I've never been so frightened.'

'I told you, it wasn't me. The police got a tip-off that he was coming here today, so they got me out of the house and substituted their own man. He was wearing a Kevlar vest in case the intruder got in a lucky shot before he was captured.'

'He wore what?' she asked, bewildered.

'It's a kind of body armour which is five times stronger than steel.'

Gaelle shook her head. 'You read about this kind of thing in the newspapers, but it hardly seems real.'

'It's real enough,' Dan said tersely. 'Now you see why I couldn't risk letting you hang around me.'

'I thought it was because you didn't want to see me again,' she admitted. 'Why didn't you tell me what was the matter?'

There was a long silence before he said, 'Scott thought you might be working with the terrorists.'

'I know. I overheard the two of you talking about it the other night.'

'Yet you still came back here.'

'You didn't believe I was a spy,' she reminded him.

'It's crazy, but I was sure you weren't, even though in my business, everybody is suspect. Not long ago, a bomb was carried on to a plane by a pregnant chambermaid who thought she was taking some antiques to her lover in Tel Aviv. But you were different.' He laughed self-deprecatingly. 'Which is the sort of ridiculous logic that can get a man killed.'

'Do I make you illogical?' she asked innocently.

'You make me crazy,' he admitted. 'I've never met anyone like you before.'

Thrilled by his admission, she nestled against him. He wasn't indifferent to her, but had been protecting her from the danger which had threatened him. 'I'm glad,' she said happily.

He tilted her face up to his. 'Why did you come back this morning?'

'To give you something.'

'Then I'll collect it now.' Before she could explain about the T-shirt, he silenced her with a kiss that sent tongues of fire racing along her veins. She gloried in the feel of his plundering mouth and gasped with pleasure as his hand slid inside her blouse. The urgency of his caresses told her how much he had been bottling up his feelings. With the danger past, he could give his passion free rein. 'Oh, Dan!' she whispered, clasping him to her.

He hooked a leg over hers and his lips roved over her eyebrows and down her face to her throat, stirring her senses to vibrant life. The message on his lips was one of demand, and she responded willingly until they were both on fire with longing. The need to be part of him was overpowering.

Dan felt it too, and slid her blouse off her shoulders so he could kiss her swelling breasts. Suddenly they felt too hot and heavy for the confinement of her bra. Feverishly, Gaelle combed her fingers through his close-cropped hair, the bristly feel of it sending tingling sensations down her fingers. He had called himself Cassius, and another reference came into her thoughts. Such men were dangerous. Dan was more than dangerous to her. He was an addiction, a fever in her blood. She doubted whether she could ever be free of his spell, even if she could conceive of wanting such a thing. 'I love you, Dan.' There, she had finally said aloud what her heart had concealed from her until this second.

He lifted passion-drugged eyes to her. 'No, don't say it, even in jest.'

'Why not, if it's true?' Gaelle wound her legs around his powerful thigh, trapping it and eliciting a sharp breath of response. 'I haven't said it until now, not even to myself, but I think I've loved you since we met in the mountains.'

'No!' His rasping denial caught her by surprise, as did his sudden shift of position. Bereft of his touch, her skin felt chilled.

She stared up at him. 'What's wrong with loving you?'

His clothes were dishevelled and his hair was spiky from her touch. He smoothed it down with a savage gesture. 'Everything's wrong with it. You don't even know me.'

'Then tell me about yourself,' she beseeched him. 'I already know what sort of work you do. I admit it frightens me, for your sake as much as mine, but I can cope with it. I'm not afraid.'

'Which shows how little you know about international terrorism,' he said flatly. 'You should be quaking in your boots. They'll stop at nothing to promote their causes. They'll turn children into walking bombs, use innocent women as unwitting couriers and worse. Doesn't it scare you? It should.'

'Why are you doing this?' Gaelle asked wildly. The memory of the black-clad man stalking Dan was still vivid in her mind. She felt the colour drain from her face and the trembling start afresh, sending shudders through her whole body. She fought them. 'You can't scare me away, Dan,' she said, though her voice shook, belying her brave words. 'I won't go.'

'You wanted to know all about me.' His voice dripped sarcasm. 'What more do I have to tell you?'

'I didn't want to know *about* you,' she corrected him, finding strength in her feelings for him. 'I want to know *you*. It isn't the same thing at all.'

Despair darkened his green eyes. 'In my case, it is, because what I do is all there is. There isn't any me to know.'

She felt the chasm widening between them, and ached for a way to reach him before it became too wide to cross with words. 'You aren't making sense,' she sighed.

Dan spread his hands wide in a gesture of defeat. 'How much more plainly can I put it? There isn't any me to know because even I don't know who I am.'

Her sense of panic increased. 'I still don't understand.'

He swung around, presenting an unforgiving

expanse of back to her, the fabric of his shirt tautening over rippling muscles. When he spoke, Gaelle could hardly hear him. 'I was a month old when the authorities found me in a bus shelter. They were never able to trace my family.' He turned his pain-racked gaze full on to her. 'Do you know what that means? I could be anyone from anywhere.'

'It still doesn't matter to me,' she insisted, frightened by the intensity of his expression.

His wide mouth twisted into a sneer. 'Doesn't it? What about genetic disease, inherited insanity, criminal tendencies? We could even be related by blood—I have no way of knowing.'

'Was that the warning you tried to give me at Megalong?'

'He nodded. 'I tried, but not hard enough, it seems. You got under my skin, despite all the reasons why I shouldn't have let it happen.'

'Love isn't something you allow, it just happens. We can't always choose it.'

'But we can choose what we do about it.'

Gaelle could hardly force the question out for fear that she already knew the answer. 'What do you choose to do about it?'

'What can I do? I can't love you when I don't know what the consequences might be. I have to let you go.'

'That's your choice. Mine is different.'

'It can't be!' Dan exploded. 'Haven't you heard a word I said? I could be anybody. Come with me.'

He caught her by the wrist and propelled her through the beautiful rooms to what must be his bedroom. It was as ruggedly masculine as Dan himself. Navy corduroy covered the walls, contrasting with the white cane and rattan furniture. A vast bed was set on a carpeted platform opposite a wall of mirrors which covered built-in wardrobes. Beyond a set of stained timber doors, Gaelle glimpsed an en-suite bathroom.

Reaching the bed, Dan thrust her on to it and she sprawled there, bewildered by the change in him. He had become hard and cold, already making good his vow not to love her. But he couldn't stop her loving him, could he?

Seeing his grim expression as his mirror-image marched towards him, she knew her first doubts. Could he make her hate him because he willed it? He was apparently going to try. 'What are you doing?' she asked in a tense whisper.

At the wardrobe, he halted and swung around. 'I could take you in the most brutal way I could devise. You'd change your mind about me then.'

She suppressed a shudder. 'No, Dan!'

'But I won't,' he went on as if she hadn't spoken. 'Because somehow, you'd turn it into romantic love, and that's a luxury I can't afford. So I have to convince you that any involvement between us is wrong.'

'But you were willing to marry me when I was having your baby. Surely that was wrong too, by your rules?'

'That was different. After what happened to me, I couldn't let a child come into the world not knowing its father. Besides, the damage had already been done. I couldn't make it any worse.

Tears of anger and humiliation sprang to her eyes

and she blinked them away. 'You make it sound so sordid!'

'No, it wasn't sordid, but it was a mistake, and I take my share of the blame.'

'Why must there be any blame?' she cried. 'I know it's terrible not to know where you come from, but you've only considered the worst possibilities. There are others.'

Dan's green eyes flashed as he loomed over her. 'I suppose you know all about it, fitting your nice little family trees together piece by piece. Can you imagine what it's like not to have a single piece to fit together? To walk the streets looking at every face and wondering if it belongs to your mother or father? You say it's terrible, but you don't know the half of it. It's sheer agony, and it lasts a lifetime. I could never put a child of mine through such torment. Marrying you would have been a huge risk, but I was prepared to take it for the child's sake.'

'But not for mine or your own?' As she said it, Gaelle knew it was true. Dan cared for her, maybe even loved her. But it wasn't going to change his mind. 'Are you sure this isn't just an excuse?' she asked, flinching as she saw his rage deepen.

'What the hell does that mean?'

'What it says.' She feared his anger, but she had nothing left to lose, and she knew she could bear his fury more readily than his indifference. 'I think you're scared!' she flung at him.

'You bet I am,' he ground out. 'Scared of unleashing an unknown set of genes on a new generation!'

Defiantly, Gaelle lifted her head, ignoring the tears

that glittered behind her angry gaze. 'That isn't what I mean. I think you're scared of the commitment, so you use your history as a shield. This way, you get to love 'em and leave 'em with a clear conscience.'

Her barb had gone home, she saw when his green eyes hardened. 'Very well, Miss Know-all! Come here.'

He pulled her across to the cavernous wardrobe and flung back the doors so hard that they rattled on their tracks. Then he hauled a box down from a top shelf and threw it on to the bed so that the contents spilled over the quilt. Shaken by the force of his anger, she looked at the contents. 'Baby clothes?'

'Yes, baby clothes,' he echoed bitterly. 'They're the so-called shield you accuse me of using.'

Since he left her no choice, she touched the tiny garments with fingers that shook. 'Yours?' she asked in a barely audible tone.

'My entire history in a box.' He thrust one of the garments into her hands. More than thirty years old, it had once been white and was now yellowed, but carefully preserved. Gaelle smoothed the tiny garment out and held it up. Made of cheap cotton, it was the kind of baby dress sold in thousands by chains stores. The only difference was the edging of fine shuttle lace worked around the tiny collar.

She fingered it, admiring the skill of its maker. Someone had spent hours making the lace trim for the cheap dress. It gave her a sense of kinship with Dan's mother, whoever she was. Gaelle pictured her working the minute knots and airy picots of the snowflake-like edging while she waited for her time to come. 'Were there no other labels or marks?' she asked Dan.

'Just what you see there,' he said flatly.

She returned her attention to the dress. The only mark of any kind was the name Daniel, written in pencil on the yoke. The writing, now barely legible, suggested that Dan's mother had intended to embroider over the word later. Gaelle had done the same thing herself, but the faded pencil lines were no help as a clue. 'The lace is distinctive,' she suggested timidly.

'There's no point getting carried away by a bit of trimming,' he assured her. 'The police and welfare tried everything to trace my mother through that garment. She left no note, nothing. If it hadn't been for the pencil marks, I wouldn't have known my first name. As it is, my surname, Buckhorn, comes from the street where I was found. Some history, huh?'

'But weren't you adopted?' she asked.

'Fostered,' he corrected her. 'The Lawsons couldn't adopt me legally without knowing more about my background.'

So she'd been wrong about his relationship to Scott Lawson. Scott's family had fostered Dan, not the other way around. Still clutching the dress, she sank on to the bed. 'None of this need change how we feel about each other, surely?' she persisted.

'It should. We'd never know what we were passing on to our children.'

'It didn't stop us before.'

Some of the hardness left his expression, and she watched him wage an internal war with himself. 'I told you, that was a mistake.'

'But we made it. We can't unmake it. You know you're special to me, Dan. I can't make the feeling go away because you tell me to.'

'Then *I'll* go away,' he offered. 'There's plenty of work for me in Europe once I get the bugs ironed out of this computer program.'

Gaelle felt the wetness on her cheeks, but didn't give a damn whether he saw it this time. She felt helpless, defeated by a woman she'd never met, who had abandoned her baby over thirty years ago. 'What can I say to make you change your mind?' she pleaded.

'Nothing,' he stated, but she heard the catch in his voice and knew that he wasn't as sure of his decision as he wanted her to believe. He was so determined to do the right thing that he was prepared to destroy them both. 'Unless, of course, you can find the owner of that.' He gestured towards the tiny garment she was still holding.

She met his challenging gaze, her eyes glistening but unblinking. 'Would it make a difference to us if I did find something?' she asked.

'It isn't possible. Too many experts have tried and failed.'

She fought the excitement that welled up inside her. 'Maybe they were experts in the wrong things.'

For a moment, Dan's eyes glowed fever-bright, then the hope vanished and his expression grew cold. 'Don't make promises you can't keep.'

'I'm not making promises nor asking for any. I only need to know that my efforts could make a difference.'

He expelled a hissing breath. 'It could make a difference.'

Gaelle indicated the baby dress. 'May I borrow this

for a while?' she asked.

'Take it—not that it'll do any good.'

Her lips parted in a faint smile. 'We'll see.'

CHAPTER SEVEN

AT HOME alone, some of Gaelle's confidence evaporated. The authorities had exhausted every avenue in their efforts to find Dan's parents. What made her think she could do better after such a long time?

Pensively she handled the yellowed baby dress, trying unsuccessfully to conjure up an image of its owner. It was hard to imagine how Dan must feel, with a yawning chasm where his past should be. If only she could do something to help!

The dress gave no clues, and besides, the police had already tried to trace it. Still, the lace that edged the collar nagged at her, familiar yet elusive. She reached for her magnifying glass.

Magnified, the lace was even more exquisite. A central ring surrounded by picots formed the basic design, but the method interested her more. She recognised it as needle tatting, first seen in the 1830s. It was unusual in that a needle was used to join the rings in single-thread, creating an airy, scalloped effect. Gaelle compared it with her own lace. Hers was made using a shuttle, the rings joined with chains. On the older lace, the single threads had been crocheted over to make a heading which was attached to the dress.

It was the work of an expert, recognisable only to

another enthusiast. Like Dan, the police could have dismissed it as a mere trimming, of no consequence. To Gaelle, the design was distinctive and somehow familiar. She screwed her face up in concentration. Where had she seen it before?

It came back to her in a rush. The design had won a prize in an exhibition by the Lacemakers' Guild in the 1950s. It had been pointed out to her when she was researching her lecture for the evening college.

She jumped to her feet, trying to control her excitement. She'd photocopied material about the exhibition from the Guild's files. Perhaps she had a picture of the winning designs.

Moments later she held the photocopy in trembling hands, hardly able to believe her luck. Her eyes raced across the pictures, searching for names. Her heart sank. They were all grouped together at the foot of the page, with no way to match the names with the designs.

'There has to be a way,' she said aloud. Her genealogy research had taught her that most mysteries yielded to patient research. She sat down at the table and spread the photocopy in front of her.

Logic told her that Dan's mother was probably not married; a married woman was unlikely to have abandoned her child. So she could safely cross out Mrs Winter and Mrs Appleyard. That left Miss B Woolcott-Jones of Sydney and Miss M Taylor of Bundanoon. She took a deep breath. Was one of them Dan's real mother?

On a hunch, she telephoned the Guild's office in the historic Rocks area of Sydney Cove. They had no listing for M Taylor, but it appeared that Miss

Woolcott-Jones was still listed. 'One of our longest-serving members,' the secretary told her proudly. 'She joined the Guild in 1915 and has been with us ever since.'

Miss Woolcott-Jones must be in her seventies now, Gaelle surmised. She couldn't be Dan's mother. Maybe it was a false lead, after all. Miss Taylor could still be the right person, but how could Gaelle find her?

She was pondering the problem when her doorbell rang. She opened the door and her heart gave a lurch of joyous recognition. 'Dan!' she exclaimed. So he couldn't stay away, after all. 'Come in,' she urged. He stepped inside and closed her door, fastening the security chain with care. His grim manner unnerved her. 'What is it? What's the matter?' she asked anxiously.

'I just had a call from the police. The man they caught outside my house says he has an accomplice who'll take over where he left off.'

Her hand flew to her mouth. 'Oh, no!'

'There's worse,' he went on. 'They're threatening to kidnap you as a way of stopping me.'

Gaelle went cold with shock. 'What can we do?'

'Very little, I'm afraid. I wanted a guard put on your house, but the police haven't the manpower. In any case, they feel sure the man is bluffing.'

'But what if he isn't?'

'That's why I'm here. I got you into this, and I'd never forgive myself if you got hurt because of me.'

'So this visit wasn't your choice.' Gaelle couldn't keep the disappointment out of her voice.

'No, it wasn't. It only confirms that you're better

off without me.' Dan grasped her shoulders and faced her, his expression pleading. 'I have an unknown past and an uncertain future. You deserve better, can't you see that?'

His hands radiated warmth through her blouse, but she welcomed his touch, craved it after being apart from him for a matter of hours. How could she face a lifetime of such deprivation? 'Surely I'm the one to judge what's best for me?' she said.

'Not where I'm concerned. I hate myself for leading you astray at Megalong before you fully understood what you were getting into. If I could take those hours back, I would.'

Her eyes searched his face. 'Would you?'

Dan looked down at her, his gaze unfathomable. 'I should.'

Which wasn't the same thing at all.

While she followed his instructions and kept well clear of the windows, he searched the house and garden, then locked all the windows and doors. 'You should be safe in here until the police can confirm their prisoner's story,' he told her.

'Do you think he's bluffing?' she asked.

'Probably. The man belongs to a group of Middle Eastern fanatics who aren't known for their patience. If there really was an accomplice, we'd have heard from him by now.'

Gaelle's voice took on a slightly hysterical edge. 'Am I supposed to wait here till I find out?'

'*We* are going to wait here,' Dan amended. 'I don't intend to leave you until the police give the all-clear.'

Only hours before, she would have been thrilled to have him spend the night under her roof. Now she wasn't sure. In his haste to reach her, he had dressed carelessly in grey corduroy trousers and a black polo-necked sweater, and the lower half of his face was dark with stubble. He looked forbidding. Such men are dangerous, she remembered. And he brought danger with him. Why couldn't he have come to her willingly, instead of like this?

She half turned away and he caught her arm, pulling her closer. 'I'm sorry, Gaelle—I didn't want it to be like this.'

She looked at him sorrowfully. 'Neither did I.'

He insisted she should go on with her work, but it was difficult to concentrate when every nerve in her body vibrated in response to his nearness. She hadn't told him what she was working on, for fear of disappointing him if she failed. He had taken it for granted that she was engaged in her genealogical work.

Finally she turned off her computer. How could she work when every lift of her head brought Dan into her field of vision? He sat in her father's old armchair, with his long legs stretched out in front of him as he did complex calculations on a clipboard he'd borrowed from Gaelle. A sea of crumpled paper lay around him. She came up behind him and touched his shoulder, jumping when he gained his feet in an instant.

'Don't sneak up on me, ever!' he commanded.

His lightening-fast move made her jump back. 'I didn't think—I'm sorry.'

'So am I.' He smoothed his hair back in a gesture which she was fast indentifying with him. 'I'm a bit jumpy at present.'

Gaelle affected a bright tone, although her heart was thumping. She was on edge too. 'I thought, since we can't go out, I'd cook dinner for us here,' she explained.

'Don't go to any trouble,' he insisted.

She nodded in apparent agreement, but her mind was already sifting through her collection of recipes. She had fresh mushrooms in the refrigerator, so she decided to make a tagliatelle with mushrooms and cream, butterfly steaks of pork from her freezer, with home-made coffee ice-cream for dessert.

Dan came into the kitchen to watch her cook. 'Do you enjoy doing this?' he asked.

'I love cooking, especially for an audience. Don't you?'

'I'm on the move so much that I eat out more often than in.'

'Then this will be a treat for you.'

'Don't, Gaelle!' he said sharply. 'Cosy evenings at home don't suit my life-style, so there's no point getting ideas.'

It was precisely what she had been doing, she acknowledged unhappily. He must have read her mind. 'Don't worry, I won't,' she said over her shoulder, as she prepared the pasta. She determined not to let him make her angry. 'How's the computer program going?'

'It should be finished in a couple of days.'

So soon? Gaelle's head was bent over the chopping board, so Dan didn't see the distress this news caused her. 'What will you do then?' she asked without looking up.

'I've been offered another assignment tightening

up security at some sheikh's kingdom along the Persian Gulf. He wants to pay me in oil wells and women. I might let him.'

He was baiting her, trying to make her see the futility of pursuing a relationship with him. But she wasn't giving up so easily. She ladled the pasta into a serving dish and spooned the creamy sauce on top, then lifted the pork steaks on to their plates. 'Shall we eat in here?' she said.

Dan pulled the blinds down, shielding them from the garden. 'This should be fine.'

He enjoyed his meal, she was sure. But he made no comment. Only the clean plates at the end gave him away. Gaelle served their coffee, then sat back. 'Are all your jobs like this Persian Gulf thing?' she asked him.

'Mostly. I have to spend some time at the location, usually incognito, so I can zero in on the weak spots in their security and suggest ways it can be tightened up. These days, most airports have their own security forces who work with the international intelligence services, so a lot of factors have to be co-ordinated to make the thing work.'

'It's all hush-hush, I suppose?'

He nodded. 'As fast as anti-terrorist measures are installed they find ways to get around them, so it doesn't pay to talk about what we're doing. And sometimes they want us to find their devices.'

Gaelle took a sip of coffee. 'Why would they?'

Dan's faced remained impassive. 'Some explosives are fitted with anti-handling devices, designed to blow up anyone who tries to disarm them.'

'Oh, my God!'

'Exactly,' he said drily.

She went cold from head to foot, then realised that he was trying to frighten her again. He was succeeding admirably. She mustered a smile. 'How interesting!'

'You don't give up, do you?' he demanded, surprising her.

'What?'

'When I talk about security men triggering their own deaths, you're supposed to turn pale and run a mile. Not blink and say, "How interesting".'

'I am turning pale inwardly. Who wouldn't? But I refuse to run away. You face up to the hazards of your work well enough.'

'It's easy when you've nothing to lose.' He reached for the coffee jug and replenished his cup. 'Since you refuse to be scared off, let's talk about you for a change. Tell me about your work.'

Sure that he would find it boring compared with what he did, Gaelle gave him a much-abridged account of how she traced people's family histories. 'It isn't always straightforward,' she explained. 'There might be several convicts of the same name, who arrived in Australia at about the same time, and I have to match the right ancestor with a client. Often they don't know when a parent or grandparent was born or died. That's where shipping records, parish records and census rolls come in handy.'

Dan sat forward and cupped his chin in one hand. 'It sounds fascinating.'

'It can be real detective work at times. At others, it's drudgery. Some day I hope to have time to trace my own family tree.' She laughed. 'It's the only one I haven't done yet!'

At the mention of her family tree, she saw a shadow pass across his features. She longed to tell him what she had learned about the lace. Knowing how much it meant to him, and how he would be hurt if she failed to learn any more, she kept silent. 'This must be boring you,' she said, standing up and reaching for the dishes.

Dan didn't contradict her. Stretching, he asked if he could use her shower. 'I left home in rather a hurry,' he explained.

'Then you're in luck,' she told him. 'I have a man's bathrobe on hand which you're welcome to use.'

She waited for him to ask how she came by it, but when he didn't she offered the explanation herself. 'I bought it for Nick's birthday, but we broke up before I could give it to him. It's brand new.' From a drawer, she took out the robe, still in its cellophane wrapper, and gave it to him.

Impassively he accepted it. 'Thank Nick for me when you see him.'

Frustration made her want to stamp her foot at him, but he had already disappeared into the bathroom. He knew perfectly well that she wasn't seeing Nick any more. Another of his not-so-subtle hints? Crossly, she rattled the dishes together in the sink and plonked them noisily on to the drainer. If Dan heard her he gave no sign. Above the splash of the water, Gaelle could hear him, singing at the top of his voice, oblivious to her mood.

He stayed under the shower for a long time, and she used the opportunity to slip into a prettily patterned, button-through dress trimmed with more of her own lace. Dan was singing an operatic aria, she noticed. What an extraordinary man he was, making his living by devising ways to trap terrorists, jumping out of planes for fun, and singing opera in the shower! For the first time, she understood the term self-made man. Dan had made himself from scratch. With no life history, he had moulded himself out of his own unique clay. A shudder of longing shook her. He was like a magnet which could attract or repel her, depending on which way it turned. The phone shrilled and she tensed, wondering if she should answer it. Her glance flickered to the bathroom, but there was no response from Dan.

Gaelle picked it up. 'Hello?'

'Miss Maxwell, this is Detective Barr. We met this morning.'

Relief flooded through her. 'I'm glad it's you, Detective.'

'Has something happened?' he asked.

'When the phone rang, I was afraid it might.'

She heard him chuckle in understanding. 'I see. Well, you can relax. Our man has admitted he was working alone and all our enquiries confirm it. His talk about an accomplice was bravado. I think he hoped to bargain with the information, and changed his mind when we didn't buy it. I'm sorry to call so late, but I'm sure you'll sleep easier for knowing.'

Fervently, she agreed with him and hung up. Anxious to share the news with Dan, she pushed open the bathroom door, expecting to find him still under the shower with the screen closed. But the water was off, and she stopped short as she caught sight of him swathed in a towel, in the act of thrusting a comb through his glistening hair. He was magnificent, and his mahogany-tanned skin gleamed wetly. Her eyes followed the path of the rivulets as they disappeared beneath the towelling.

Catching sight of her in the mirror, he swung around, and his intake of breath echoed hers. When the phone rang, she had been about to fasten her dress. Only the middle two buttons were closed. The rest swung open, revealing the deep cleft between her breasts and a breathtaking amount of tanned thigh. They took a half-step towards each other, then stopped. Gaelle watched Dan fight a battle with himself and lose. Two more strides brought him to her, and he swore softly as he crushed her against his flint-hard body.

Eagerly she returned his embrace, feeling the welcome roughness of his skin teasing hers. The towel concealed nothing of his response to her. An answering warmth flowed through her, driving all thoughts from her mind.

They were half-way to her bedroom before she remembered why she had come into the bathroom. 'Dan, I . . .'

He kissed her tenderly, his arm warm and heavy around her shoulders. 'I know,' he misinterpreted her anxiety. 'It's too soon after the baby. But I only want to hold you and feel the warmth of you beside me. I want to take these memories away with me when I go.'

When I go . . . the prospect filled her with anguish, driving from her mind the news she had been about to tell him. All she could think about was how empty her life would be without him. She clung to him, storing up the memory of his embrace, as they walked towards the bed.

He was still holding her when his breathing slowed and he drifted into sleep. His arm rested across her breasts, but she was glad of its weight to remind her that he was still here.

Carefully, to avoid disturbing him, she turned her head, and smiled as her gaze was rewarded by the sight of his dark head cushioned against her shoulder. In repose, he looked much less forbidding, with his long, dark lashes pillowed on sculptured cheeks, and his generous mouth relaxed into a half-smile. The cynicism was gone and, with the green eyes veiled, his usual wariness was absent. He didn't look at all dangerous now.

Nestling against him, Gaelle gave herself up to sleep.

'Good morning, sleepyhead.' She opened sleep-drugged eyes to find him standing over her. 'I made you some coffee.'

Like a cat, she stretched languorously, then sat up and took the offered cup. Over the rim, she studied him, noting the contrasts between Dan-asleep and Dan-awake. Now, dressed only in his grey trousers, his massive chest bare, he looked panther-like. The sense of power, barely leashed, was back in every controlled movement as he prowled around the room, picking up the clothes they had discarded the night before.

'Would you open the blind, please?' she asked.

'When you're up and dressed. We don't know who might be watching the house. There's no sense in presenting yourself as a target.'

'But I'm not . . .' she blurted out. Damn! She had forgotten to tell him about the detective's call. He thought they were still in danger. Biting her lip, she told him now.

His angry reaction caught her unawares. 'What the hell are you playing at, keeping something like that to yourself?'

'I didn't plan to,' Gaelle defended herself. 'When I saw you in the bathroom, I just forgot everything else.'

'I should be flattererd, I suppose,' he retorted, his tone bitingly sarcastic. 'But I can see through your clever game.'

She was genuinely puzzled. 'What game?'

'I wouldn't fall in with your romantic scheme, so you decided to use last night as an excuse. You knew if you'd told me the danger was past, I would have packed up and left.'

Shocked, she stared at him. 'I didn't keep quiet to trick you into staying. I'm not that desperate for a man!'

Conflicting emotions chased themselves across Dan's face. Finally, reason won. 'I didn't mean to suggest you were sex-starved, Gaelle—God, I don't know what got into me even to suggest it! It won't happen again.'

He picked up his sweater and shrugged it on, then combed his thick hair into order. She watched him impassively, still hurt by his unwarranted accusation. It took some of the joy out of having him here. 'Are you leaving now?' she asked tonelessly.'

'It would be best. Now the danger's past, I have no

reason to stay.'

Her self-control ebbed away. She couldn't let him walk out of her house and her life. Where he was concerned, she had no pride. 'Stay because I want you to,' she begged. 'Isn't it reason enough?'

Dan turned from the mirror and pocketed the comb. 'It's the best reason for me to go. Haven't you seen enough of what life with me would be like to know when to quit? I have no pedigree to offer you, only a good chance you'd one day get a telegram saying sorry but I was blown to bits somewhere along the Persian Gulf.'

'Don't, please!' she begged.

Taking the cup from her, he grasped her wrists so she was forced to look at him. 'I'm not saying it just to frighten you. I want you to see that loving me is the worst thing you could do. I can't make you happy. Don't love me, Gaelle, for your own sake.'

'But I do,' she whispered abjectly. 'Tell me how to stop.'

'I've given you every reason I can. What more can I do?'

'I don't know. I only know I can't let you walk away because of some stupid hang-ups. I don't care about the past, or the danger. I only care about you.'

'Then there's nothing I can do to change your mind.'

He started towards the door, and she knew she was going to lose him if she didn't do something quickly. 'Dan, wait! I . . . I may have found out something about where you come from.'

His knuckles gripping the doorknob were pale. 'If this is another scheme . . .'

'No, it isn't. The clue is in the lace trimming around the baby clothes.'

'But the police checked into the clothes. Anybody could have bought that gown from any one of thousands of stores around the country.'

'But anyone couldn't have made the lace,' Gaelle persisted. 'It's an original design by a traditional method which very few people know. I wouldn't have recognised it myself but for some research I did recently for a lecture.'

She could hardly bear the force of the gaze he turned on her. It raked her like a laser beam until she lowered her lashes against its intensity. 'Do you know who made it?' he asked.

'Not yet. The same design won a prize at an exhibition in 1952, so it could be the person who entered it.'

Dan sucked in his breath. '1952 is the year I was born.'

'Then I must be on the right track, Oh, Dan, if only . . .'

'No, don't!' he ordered, so viciously that she flinched. 'Don't start to hope yet, until you know more.'

The order was directed at her, but she knew he was giving it equally to himself. 'I'll try,' she agreed, knowing it wouldn't be easy—for either of them.

He nodded tautly. 'What's your next step?'

'One of the prizewinners is still a member of the Lacemakers' Guild—a Miss Bertha Woolcott-Jones. She's in her seventies,' Gaelle added as she saw his eyes lighten. Despite his injunction, he was allowing himself to hope, she recognised, and prayed that she wouldn't have to disappoint him. She almost wished she had kept silent, but then he would be gone. 'I'm seeing the lady this morning,' she added. 'The Guild contacted her for me and assured her I was a bona-fide researcher. Why don't you come with me?'

He wavered. 'I would, but the police are expecting me to help with the investigation. We should be finished by lunch time. I could meet you back here.'

She nodded eagerly and he crossed the room to kiss her, his hands lingering on her shoulders as if it was an effort to release her. Her spirits lightened as she heard him leave. This time, it wasn't goodbye. He was coming back.

Bertha Woolcott-Jones turned out to be a surprise. For a woman in her seventies, she was full of life and laughter. Her cornflower-blue eyes sparkled behind fashionable spectacles and her silver hair was carefully styled. She lived in a town house in Balmain, and welcomed Gaelle like a long-lost daughter.

Before Gaelle could broach the reason for her visit, she was plied with tea and spiced apple muffins. 'I wish I could say I cooked them, but we have a charming French place near here where I buy them,' Miss Woolcott-Jones confided to Gaelle.

Around a bite of cake, Gaelle nodded. 'They're delicious, Miss Woolcott-Jones.'

The woman laughed. 'Call me Bertha, please—the other is too much of a mouthful!' She leaned closer. 'The Guild people tell me you're a lacemaker as well as a genealogist.'

'That's right. My grandmother taught me tatting

when I was little. I've been doing it ever since.'

Bertha looked approving. 'It's good to know the old skills are carried on. When I heard you were coming, I got out some things I thought would interest you.'

Although she longed to ask about the 1952 exhibition, Gaelle bided her time. Bertha obviously enjoyed visitors, especially when they shared her lifelong hobby, so it was little enough to do, showing an interest in her collection.

Polite attention soon turned to genuine enthusiasm as Bertha brought out worn, fragile copies of the old *Woman's Mirror* and some yellowing pages from an old *Australian Home Beautiful*. 'I still make Norma Benporath's designs,' she said, indicating the treasured articles. 'She made all her own samples to illustrate her patterns, and the embroidery was done by her mother.' She clucked her tongue. 'I don't do so much tatting now, with my arthritis. Why don't you have these patterns?'

'I couldn't, they're much too valuable,' Gaelle demurred. But the fragile sheets of paper were thrust into her hands and she could only murmur her thanks.

'Now, I mustn't keep you talking,' Bertha reminded herself. 'What did you want to see me about? Some research of yours?'

Gaelle tried to keep the excitment out of her voice. 'In a way. I'm trying to track down the designer of this.'

Bertha took the baby's dress from her and peered closely at the lace-trimmed collar. 'It's beautiful!' she exclaimed.

'I know. I believe that design won a prize at the

Guild's 1952 exhibition, along with one of yours.'

'Ah yes, I remember being so pleased and proud. Mary was too.'

Something tight clamped itself around Gaelle's chest. 'Mary?' she queried.

Bertha nodded, her eyes clouding as she remembered. 'Mary Taylor, a dear little thing from the country. She came up especially for the exhibition. I worried about her travelling so near her time, but she said her husband was meeting her in Sydney, so I suppose it was all right.'

'She wasn't from Bundanoon, was she?' Gaelle asked with studied casualness.

'I couldn't have given you the name, but now that you mention it, I think she was. Yes, definitely. I wonder how she got on with the little one.'

Disappointment pierced Gaelle. 'You didn't see her after the exhibition?'

'I'm afraid not. I was taken ill myself afterwards and had to go to hospital, so I couldn't visit her. I was in Royal North Shore and she went to the Little Sisters Private Hospital, so we weren't even in the same place.'

Gaelle sent a fervent prayer of thanks winging upwards. 'The Little Sisters? Oh, Bertha, I can't thank you enough!'

The woman blinked. 'Did I say something useful?'

'Oh, you did, you did!' She felt like hugging her. Instead she stood up, trying not to appear too anxious to be on her way. 'Thanks for the morning tea and the patterns. I shall treasure them.'

'You're more than welcome,' Bertha assured her. 'Do visit me again and we'll talk lacemaking some more. Even if I can't do it as well as I used to, I like seeing what others have made.'

'I'd love to,' Gaelle promised. On impulse, she planted a light kiss on the woman's cheek. 'Thanks again!'

She could hardly wait to get home and think through her next step. She knew she wasn't being rational or methodical, as befitted a trained researcher, but her heart was so overflowing with joy, she could barely think straight.

There was no sign of Dan when she reached home, and she was pleased. She had more checking to do before he arrived, and then she would be able to tell him the wonderful news that his real mother could be a Mary Taylor of Bundanoon.

Even the township seemed providential. Gaelle's father had been born there, leaving it for Sydney in his teens. Gaelle herself had only driven through the place, but recalled it as a peaceful rural centre with glorious scenery. She was sorry now that she hadn't learned more about the town from her father before he died. But it was too late. Her mother couldn't help. She came from Queensland and had been nursing in Sydney when she'd met Gaelle's father. Now she was remarried and living in New Zealand, too far away for more than occasional letters. There were no relatives left in Bundanoon, so Gaelle would have to start from scratch.

With a cup of tea at her elbow, she made herself think calmly. Mary Taylor was a common name, which was unfortunate. She blessed Bertha for remembering that the woman had gone to the Little Sisters Hospital to have her child. She could be the wrong person entirely, so Gaelle would have to proceed carefully. Even supposing she found the woman, she couldn't accuse her of abandoning her baby. Gaelle would need to be sure of her facts.

She made her first call to Jill. 'I'm not interrupting anything, am I?' she asked.

'I'm sitting with my feet up and a cup of coffee in my hand,' Jill confessed. 'I've just come in from delivering a baby, so my partner is taking my morning surgery.'

Gaelle explained what she needed. 'I thought a doctor might have better luck approaching a hospital than a layman.'

'Not necessarily,' Jill admitted. 'The Little Sisters is a nursing home now, so they may not have records going back to 1952. What reason can I give for needing them?'

Gaelle hesitated, then plunged on. 'I'm finally doing my own family tree. A girl called Mary Taylor had a baby at that hospital in 1952. She's from Bundanoon where my dad was born, and I'm trying to find out if we're related.'

'If it's for your own use, that's different,' said Jill, sounding relieved. 'I'll see what I can do.'

They talked for a few more minutes as Jill quizzed Gaelle about her recovery. She was pleased to find that her patient had suffered no lasting ill effects. 'I get depressed when I think about what happened, but I'm keeping busy,' Gaelle said.

'It's the best therapy,' Jill assured her, then she groaned. 'I have to go—I'm being paged. I don't hold out much hope that they'll have the records you need, but I'll do my best. Talk to you soon.'

Hearing a click from the other end of the line, Gaelle hung up. She was seething with impatience and was tempted to contact the hospital herself to see what she could find out. But Jill would have a much better chance of uncovering anything worth while. Gaelle would just have to wait.

To distract herself, she set about concocting a magnificent lunch for Dan when he arrived. She put a whole Atlantic salmon to bake in the oven and tossed a salad in French dressing, all the while listening for the sound of his car. Realising what she was doing, she smiled at her own foolishness. Anyone would think she was a bride, waiting for her new husband to come home from a day at the office!

The sound of the telephone interrupted her daydream and she raced to answer it. As she prayed, the caller was Jill.

'I didn't have too much trouble,' the doctor said, sounding surprised but pleased with herself. 'They don't have records as far back as 1952, but the Charge Sister was a trainee nurse in the hospital at the time. I could hardly get her off the phone! She wanted to tell me your Mary Taylor's entire life history.'

'What did you learn?' Gaelle asked breathlessly.

'The Sister recalled her because she was such a frightened little thing. To quote her, they never saw a husband, although the girl wore a wedding ring and insisted her husband would come. The nurse had to register the birth for her, since she was too confused to manage it herself.'

The tightness around Gaelle's chest threatened to strangle her. She could hardly force the words out.

'Could she remember the child's name?'
    'Yes, as it happens. It was a boy, called Daniel.'

CHAPTER EIGHT

GAELLE could hardly contain her excitement. Mary Taylor must be Dan's real mother! It was too much of a coincidence that she had given birth to a boy named Daniel at the right hospital at the right time.

Before Jill rang off, she gave Gaelle an exact date of birth and the name of her contact at the hospital in case Gaelle needed more information. She hugged the notebook against her chest and did a couple of dance steps around the kitchen. She could hardly wait to tell Dan her news. But there was no sign of his car outside, and as she watched from the window, the telephone rang again.

'Dan, where are you calling from?' she asked as she recognised his voice. The warm, velvety tones sent a thrill of anticipation through her.

'I'm still with the police,' he told her.

'Nothing's wrong, is it?'

'No, but the enquiry is taking longer than we expected. I won't make it in time for lunch after all.'

Gaelle's sense of letdown was overwelming. 'I understand. Will you be here for dinner?'

'I'll try. I must go now, this is a public phone.'

She longed to be able to tell him some of her news, but this wasn't the time or the place. 'I'll be waiting,' she said softly.

'I know. I'll be there as soon as I can.'

The line went dead. She tried to tell herself that the delay wasn't the end of the world. She would have to get used to Dan's erratic life-style, she supposed. At least she had her own work to occupy her while he was away. She was getting ahead of herself, she realised, but it was increasingly difficult to conceive of a future without Dan.

Removing the cooked salmon from the oven, she left it to cool in the refrigerator. It would make a tasty cold meal tonight. Returning to her desk, she determined to make as much progress as she could to surprise Dan when he arrived.

Her first call was to a friend at the registry of births. The privacy restrictions sometimes made it harder to trace living people than long-dead ones. She hoped her professional reputation would help her overcome any difficulties.

After her friend had made exhaustive checks of the correct index, Gaelle was no further forward. 'There must be a Daniel Taylor,' she insisted. 'He was registered by the nurse at the hospital, so I know it must be there.'

Her friend clucked her tongue sympathetically. 'You've been through this as often as I have, Gaelle. If it was easy, nobody would need your services. Several Daniel Taylors are listed for 1952, but they don't fit the other requirements you mention. Have you checked under the mother's surname yet? If she was single, he would have been registered under her name.'

'Taylor *is* his mother's surname,' Gaelle confirmed. 'I assumed his mother was single, but maybe I'm wrong. Thanks, Jenny. You've been a great help.'

She could hear the puzzlement in her friend's voice as they said goodbye. Gaelle felt her sense of adventure rekindling. Now she had to find out the name of Daniel's father. The chance was remote, since the nurse hadn't even met Mary's husband. Maybe he did exist, after all. Again, Gaelle picked up the phone and cradled it against her shoulder as she readied her notepad.

The Charge Sister sounded wary when she came to the phone. 'I already told Doctor Barwick everything I could remember,' she told Gaelle.

'I know. You have an amazing memory,' Gaelle enthused. 'Not many people could recall one patient out of the thousands you must have looked after since then.'

'I remember most of them,' the nurse said, thawing slightly. 'Mary Taylor stuck in my mind because she was so lost and helpless. The city scared her almost as much as having a baby. She was so nice that I wanted to make things easier for her.'

'I'm sure you did. Doctor Barwick said you even registered the baby's birth for her.'

'The poor girl didn't know where to begin, so I helped her,' the nurse confirmed. 'I used to wonder what became of her and the baby. Lots of our new mothers keep in touch, but she never did.'

Gaelle curbed her impatience. 'What a shame! You must feel like one of the family after being so involved with each new life.'

'Oh, I do,' the nurse agreed. 'It's one of the things I miss since the hospital became a nursing home. A birth is such a happy time. Not that our patients aren't happy, but it's a different stage of life. You know?'

'I know. I was hoping you could remember one more detail for me—the surname of Mary's husband.'

'I thought that was why you were enquiring!' the nurse said, sounding surprised. 'His name was the same as yours—Maxwell. I recall it because it struck me as unusual. Simpson Maxwell. You did say you were researching your own family tree?'

Swallowing the lump which had arisen in her throat, Gaelle said hastily, 'Yes, but Maxwell is a common surname, so I wanted to be sure. Thank you for your help.'

For a long time after she'd hung up, Gaelle stared at the telephone, immobilised by the shock of her discovery. Mary Taylor had given the nurse the name of Simpson Maxwell as the baby's father. Even before she checked it out, she knew what she was going to find when she went back to the registry of births. Sure enough, Dan was registered as Daniel Maxwell, son of Mary Taylor and Simpson Maxwell.

And Simpson was Gaelle's own father.

Shock drained the colour from her face and a chill gripped her. That meant Dan was her half-brother. What had they done?'

Simpson must have fathered Dan before he'd married Gaelle's mother. It was a staggering discovery. But why hadn't he married Mary Taylor? Unless he had left Bundanoon without knowing that Mary was pregnant, Gaelle realised. Her father would never have abandoned his responsibilities, she was sure.

In sudden anguish, she hurled her notebook across the room, then collapsed into helpless sobs.

Simpson's motives were less vital than the realisation that she could never have a future with Dan now. They were brother and sister; their love was forever forbidden.

This was the very outcome Dan had feared when he'd refused to give her his love. How wise he seemed now, to cut himself off from attachment for fear of the unknown past! Now they were to be punished for something that wasn't their fault and which they could never change. There was no way to undo the damage of the last few days.

Oh God, the baby! Had she miscarried because nature knew the hazards? Jill thought it was because she wasn't physically ready, but Gaelle began to wonder. She should have suspected something when she found out where Mary Taylor came from. But lots of people were born or raised in the Southern Highlands. She had never imagined anything like this.

She was unaware of the light failing as she sat staring at the walls of her study. What was she going to do? Stupidly she had wanted to solve the mystery of Dan's past so he would be hers. Now he was, but in a way neither of them wanted. Revulsion gripped her as she recalled the intimacy of her days with Dan. They seemed halcyon now, forever beyond her reach. They had loved each other innocently. Her research had destroyed that innocence for ever.

How was she to tell Dan?

She knew she was clutching at straws, but there was a slight chance that Simpson Maxwell wasn't Dan's father after all. Mary could have known him in Bundanoon, and conjured up his name rather than admit her shame. It was a slender hope, but better than none.

For the first time Gaelle found herself hoping that the records lied. She could hardly bear a future in which Dan was no more than a brother to her. She shuddered as she imagined his reaction. He would condemn himself, however unfairly. There was no way he would stay around once he knew. She didn't know which was worse—being near him and unable to love him, or the thought of never seeing him again.

Before a choice was made she had to be sure.

Moving stiffly, she switched on the lights, surprised to find that it was almost dark. As she pulled down her blinds, she noticed Dan's car turning into the driveway, and her heart gave a painful lurch. Their cosy evening was an impossibility now, until she knew beyond doubt what he was to her.

When she opened the door to him, he offered her a huge bunch of hothouse roses. 'For you.'

'They're lovely, thank you,' she said tiredly, barring the door with her body.

Dan looked at her in concern. 'Is everything all right?'

'I don't feel very well,' she admitted.

His frown deepened. 'I'll get you to bed and call Jill.'

'No!' she said so vehemently that he looked startled. 'I've already spoken to Jill and she thinks I need to rest.'

'I knew you started work too soon. All this cloak-and-dagger stuff was too much for you.'

Her smile was faint. 'You could be right. Is it over

now?'

'Yes, thank goodness. All the threats came from the one man. Now he's in custody, we have no reason to worry.'

Until next time, Gaelle thought vaguely. She held the roses against her chest, making a barrier between them. Dan was plainly puzzled when she didn't ask him in, but she couldn't have him in her house, unable to give in to the dizzying need to touch him. She looked up at him. 'I'm sorry, I don't feel like going out tonight.'

'I understand. Go to bed and we'll talk tomorrow.' Dan frowned suddenly. 'Damn, I can't. I'm seeing a client tomorrow—the sheikh I told you about. Maybe it's for the best. You look like you could use a day in bed. Why don't I call for you on Saturday and we'll take a leisurely drive somewhere?'

The attraction between them vibrated in the air until Gaelle felt as if she would melt with the need to feel his arms around her. She couldn't go on seeing him under these conditions, knowing how wrong their love might be. She shook her head. 'I'll be busy this weekend. I have to go to the country to do some research.'

'Are you sure you're up to it?'

'I'll be fine,' she assured him.

'All the same, I can't let you overtax yourself. If you must go, I insist on driving you. I'll pick you up here at nine. All right?'

The last thing she wanted was to be alone with him. But she couldn't say no without arousing his suspicions. He was already puzzled by her behaviour; she didn't want to make matters worse.

'Very well,' she agreed reluctantly. She would have to keep her distance somehow, until she knew the truth.

Dan seemed relieved by her acquiescence. 'That's my girl!'

She wanted to cry out that she wasn't his girl, as much as she longed to be. Her hands tightened around the bouquet of roses. 'I'll see you on Saturday, then.'

A smile tilted up the corners of his mouth. 'Aren't you going to kiss me goodbye? Two days is a long time.'

Her heart all but stopped. Two days was for ever, but she still couldn't kiss him the way he expected. She stood up on tiptoe and pecked at his cheek. 'Take care!'

He twisted his head so that their lips met, sending tongues of flame shooting through her body, reminding her of how much she loved him. He stepped back. 'Until Saturday, then.' He half turned, then swung back to her. 'Did you find out anything from the old lady?'

Consumed by fires of longing for him, Gaelle shook her head. 'Not yet, but she's promised to try.'

The sudden clouding of his eyes tugged at her heartstrings. 'We'll have to hope that she remembers something.'

'Yes,' she agreed, then stepped back and closed the door between them before she broke down completely in front of him. Once he had left, the house seemed cold and empty. The 'Fire Danger' sign mocked her, having swung to 'very high'—an apt measure of her situation. The scent of Dan's roses filled her nostrils and she hugged the bouquet. How many roses would he bring once he knew?

As she arranged the flowers in a vase, her thoughts whirled dizzily. She found herself thinking about her father. If only he were here to answer the myriad questions swirling in her brain! Had he been in love with Mary Taylor? Had she borne him a child, unbeknown to him? 'Oh, Dad,' she murmured. 'If it's true, how can I live without him?'

She was already acting as if Dan was her half-brother. Cutting herself off from his love with a defence mechanism, she recognised. It would be hard enough to feel like a sister towards him after all they had shared. The sooner she accepted it, the better. How she would get through the day in his company, she didn't know. Maybe a miracle would happen between now and Saturday, and she would stop loving him.

She wished she hadn't told him she was going to the country. It was a sudden impulse, born of desperation. She had to go to Bundanoon, but not with Dan, when every mile together made the eventual separation harder to bear. Now she could only pray that what she learned there would change everything.

She intended to seek out May Dreyfuss, a friend of her father's whom Gaelle knew slightly. Her father had gone to school with May. On a visit to Sydney, she had refused an invitation to stay with the Maxwells. Gaelle remembered her as a pleasant woman in her late forties or early fifties. She had been friendly and outgoing with Gaelle, but stiff and formal with Simpson Maxwell. Gaelle recalled puzzling about it at the time.

Her need for rest was no lie, but her early night did her no good. The images of Dan haunted her all night. At first light, she got up and made some tea, then sat down at her computer and went to work on a family tree which was proving difficult. Now she welcomed the challenge to keep her mind occupied.

The problem lay with a nineteenth-century birth certificate which showed that her client's forebear had married twice between the ages of nineteen and twenty, which was clearly impossible. The certificate showed the mother's name as Elizabeth Smith, formerly Mason. Smith was her married name and Wilson her single name, but where had Mason come from?

It took Gaelle most of the day, and she was cross-eyed from squinting at microfiche records, but she finally solved the mystery. Elizabeth's father was recorded on her marriage certificate as George Wilson, Stone Mason. When Elizabeth Smith's first child was registered, a clerk had taken details from her marriage certificate and copied down Mason as a surname instead of Wilson.

Satisfied, Gaelle pushed her hair back from her forehead, astonished to find that much of the day had gone. She was tired, but had saved herself from thinking about Dan for long stretches at a time.

Her gaze travelled to the old leather armchair, and she pictured him sprawled in it. Out of love, she had stored up a vivid image. She could see his long legs crossed at the ankle to reveal black ribbed socks and a glimpse of tanned calf. Mentally she followed the line of his grey trousers, stretched taut over muscular thighs, then up to his broad chest, which rose and fell with his rhythmic breathing. His head was bent so the dark hair fell over his face and his mouth was pursed in concentration. She was half-way out of her seat before she remembered that it was a mirage. Disappointment welled up inside her and she rested her head on her hands.

Her reverie was disturbed by the telephone ringing at her elbow. She was tempted to let it ring, but it persisted, so she picked it up. At the sound of the deep masculine tones, her spirits lifted, then crashed as quickly. The caller wasn't Dan. 'Hello, Nick,' she said wearily.

'Surprised to hear from me?'

'A bit. How's Geraldine?' Gaelle remembered the name of the girl who had supplanted her in Nick's affections.

'You remembered!' he chuckled. 'I owe you an apology over her. You were quite right, she didn't have an original thought in her head.'

'Did I say that?'

''Fraid so. I only told you about her to make you jealous enough to marry me, but you said she was welcome to me.'

'Oh dear! I guess we were both upset, but it worked out for the best, didn't it? How have you been, Nick?'

'Lonely,' he confessed. 'Actually, Geraldine was the first in a long line of girls. But I got tired of hearing, ''Yes, Nick'', ''No Nick'' and ''Three bags full, Nick''.'

'I thought that's what you wanted to hear.'

'Ouch!' he winced. 'Same old Gaelle—no punches

pulled! Haven't you missed me at all?'

'I did at first,' she admittted. 'But we weren't right for each other, so it was better to go on to other things.'

'Did you? Go on to other things, I mean?'

Hearing the jealousy in his voice, Gaelle almost laughed. Nick could never handle her having men friends, even if it was completely innocent. He had even suspected her male clients. 'If I have, it's my business,' she said lightly.

He was instantly contrite. 'Of course, I shouldn't pry. Forgive me?'

'Forgiven,' she said readily. 'Was there something you wanted? I'm in the middle of a project.'

'Still besotted with those family trees of yours?' he teased, but she heard the undercurrent of irritation in his tone. Nick had never understood her dedication to her work, resenting the time it took her away from him. He sensed her annoyance. 'Oops, I did it again, didn't I?'

'Yes,' she said, keeping her temper in check with an effort. She was on edge over Dan. It wasn't fair to take it out on Nick because he had called at the wrong time.

He took an audible breath. 'I'll start again. I've been given tickets to the Genesian's new play, and I hoped you'd go with me.'

The Genesian was a theatre located in a century-old converted church. Nick knew Gaelle enjoyed the atmosphere of the place. She let the silence deepen as her thoughts raced. Less than a day ago she would have turned Nick down flat, knowing that she only wanted to be with Dan. She still wanted him.

Would she ever get used to loving him from a distance? Going out with Nick might help her to accept it. 'If I agree, it's on one condition,' she said.

He was airily confident. 'Anything.'

'I'm only agreeing to go to the theatre with you. No strings?'

He paused long enough to convince her that he had hoped to rekindle their romance. Then he said heavily, 'Very well, no strings.'

'In that case, the answer is yes.'

'Good. I'll pick you up at seven tonight and we'll have supper afterwards.'

She had only agreed to attend a play with him, not to go on to dinner, but she decided to argue with him later. Her spirits were too low to tackle Nick, the original immovable object. She could always plead tiredness later. As she said goodbye and went back to her work, she thought how typical it was of Nick to assume she was free tonight. He hadn't changed, still interrupting her work without a thought, and choosing their dates without consulting her.

She began to regret saying she would go. What was the point, when she felt nothing for him? Her hand was on the telephone when she remembered why she had agreed. The sooner she made an effort to get Dan Buckhorn out of her system, the better.

By the time Nick called for her that evening, she had almost begun to believe she could. The spell was broken as soon as she opened the door. Nick looked as well groomed as ever, in a pale grey designer suit with white shirt and dark tie, but her senses remained stubbornly unmoved. She longed to see glossy dark hair where Nick's was straw-blond, bleached by sun and surf—and a little chemical help, she had long suspected. His continental background should have made him dark and suave in appearance; instead, he looked like a playboy who spent his summers in California and his winters in St Moritz. His vivid blue eyes swept over her appreciatively. 'Very nice. You're thinner, but it suits you.'

'Thank you.' Anxious not to seem provocative, Gaelle had chosen a long-sleeved challis dress in demure navy, with white tie at the neck and white buttons. She was slimmer now and the dropped-waist design emphasised it. She manage to smile at him. 'Come in, I'm almost ready.'

He looked around her living-room. 'My picture's not here.'

At the door, she paused. 'Did you think it would be?'

'You could at least pretend you were pining, for my ego's sake.'

At his conceit, which was so typical, her smile became genuine. 'Your ego doesn't need any help from me! I'll get my bag.'

'What play are they doing?' she asked as they drove to the theatre in Nick's Lotus, the low, wedge-shaped car making her feel as if she should be hurtling around a Grand Prix racetrack.

Nick's glance flicked to her, then back to the road as he overtook another vehicle. Patience wasn't his strong suit, especially when he was behind the wheel. 'They're doing a Shakespeare season,' he told her. 'Tonight, it's *Julius Caesar.*'

Gaelle's breath caught in her throat. 'Oh, no!' she

gasped.

'Something the matter?'

Hastily she shook her head. But everything was wrong. Why hadn't she asked before, then made some excuse? Instead of helping to distance herself from Dan, tonight would only rub salt in her emotional wounds.

Somehow she sat through the play and managed not to flinch, although in Caesar's speech, she heard an echo of Dan's words: 'Such men as he be never at heart's ease.' Dan had said she eased his heart by her presence. What would he say when he knew their true relationship?

Nick's voice reached her from far away. 'I said, it's over.'

With a shock, Gaelle realised that, apart from Caesar's speech, one of her favourite plays had passed her in a dream. Stiffly she gathered her things and followed Nick to his car. 'I've made reservations at the Waterfront for supper,' he told her.

The restaurant was located at Circular Quay, in an impressively restored convict-era storehouse. They were shown to a table on the terrace, overlooking the jewelled expanse of Sydney Harbour. 'Now aren't you glad we came?' asked Nick when they were seated.'

'Do you care?' she asked bluntly, tiring of humouring him.

He looked hurt. 'Of course I do. Why do you think I asked you out tonight?'

'Because I had the temerity to turn you down. You couldn't resist the challenge.'

She half expected an angry outburst, but he threw

back his head and laughed delightedly. 'Now I know what's been missing from my life—a sparring partner! You stick to your own opinions and to hell with what I think.' His eyes were ablaze as he lifted her hand and pressed his lips against it.

Gaelle was about to pull free when her gaze was arrested by a group several tables away. A dark, hawk-nosed man and a woman were talking animatedly over their meal. In between them, looking at her so hard she thought she would burst into flame, was Dan. His eyes followed her as she snatched her hand away at last. He looked murderous.

Nick asked her what she would like to eat, and was pleased when she suggested he order for them both. 'That's more like it,' his expression seemed to say. Gaelle hardly heard what he told the waiter, but magically, a vast platter of chilled seafood appeared between them and wine was poured into her glass.

'You haven't touched your meal,' Nick observed, watching her play with the fruit decorating the tray. Although she didn't look up, she knew that Dan was watching every move. Nick had a habit of touching her to emphasise his points, and she had a fair idea of how it must look to Dan—like lovers reunited. She ached to tell him it wasn't so, but couldn't bring herself to explain why she was here with Nick tonight. Not while there was still a chance she could be wrong about her relationship to Dan.

Taking a piece of succulent lobster, she chewed it mechanically. 'This is very nice,' she said.

Angrily, Nick pushed the plate away. 'No, it isn't. The whole evening was a mistake and you know it.'

With downcast eyes, she nodded. 'I know—I'm sorry.'

'Damn! I really thought there was a chance for me. I was wrong, wasn't I?'

Impulsively, she covered his hand with hers. 'It was my fault, too. I should have been more honest when you called.'

He took a long drink of wine. 'Forget it. Let's salvage what we can of the evening. We never did have a proper farewell.'

Relief made Gaelle's face relax into a smile, but it vanished as she felt the weight of Dan's appraisal on her. Moments later, a shadow darkened the table and she looked up into his impassive expression. 'Hello, Gaelle. I'm glad to see you're feeling better.'

She ignored the reference to her supposed ill-health of last night. 'Hello, Dan. This is a friend of mine, Nick Guardino. Nick, Dan Buckhorn.'

Dan gave the other man a stiff nod. 'Good evening. Gaelle has told me a lot about you.'

Nick gave her a speculative look. 'Then you have the advantage over me. I'm afraid.'

The muscles of Dan's face worked. 'I see. Well, we're close friends, so I came to ask her for a dance, if you've no objections, of course.'

To her horror, Nick gestured expansively. 'Go ahead.'

In Dan's arms, the need to mould herself against him warred with her awareness of their relationship. She was stiff and cold in his arms. He danced in silence at first, then said heavily, 'So Nick won, after all.'

'What do you mean?'

'You used me a yardstick to test your feelings for him, didn't you?'

'No!' she protested.

'Then why did you lie to me last night?'

'I didn't . . .' She began, then saw his eyes darken. 'All right, I did. I'm sorry, but I had a lot on my mind.'

'So you still haven't made a final decision?'

How could she encourage him when she might have to let him down so cruelly? If only she had the courage to tell him she was in love with Nick, the problem would be solved. But he had a right to know about his family, even if it meant he never wanted to see her again. 'No, I haven't,' she said in a low voice.

'That means there's still a chance for me.'

'Not so long ago, you didn't want one,' she reminded him. 'You practically ordered me not to love you.'

'That was before I fell in love with you myself.'

Her cry was instinctive. 'No, you mustn't!'

His hand pressed against her back, forcing them closer. Gaelle felt him move sensuously against her and willed herself not to respond. It was like trying to stem the tide. 'It's too late,' he said softly. 'For years I told myself I shouldn't marry because of the uncertainty of my past. You convinced me I was wrong. Now I have to do the same for you. Nick isn't the man for you—I am. And I have all day tomorrow to prove it to you.'

In her confusion, she'd forgotten that he was to drive her to Bundanoon. 'I want to call the trip off,' she said weakly.

Dan shook his head. 'No way. I'm not leaving the

field clear for Guardino, although he probably has a
pedigree a mile long. You said it didn't matter. Now
you're going to prove it. I mean to have you, Gaelle,
and I usually get what I want.'

CHAPTER NINE

NEXT morning, Dan's parting words still rang in her ears. What had she done? Instead of putting some distance between herself and Dan, she had made him pursue her harder. Just a few days ago she would given much to hear him say he loved her. Now it was too late.

Dancing with him had shown how dangerous the situation was. Knowing what they could be to each other, she felt her traitorous body still responding to him as wantonly as ever. She glanced at the clock. Unable to sleep, she'd been up since dawn, and felt heavy-eyed as she waited for him to collect her.

She fumbled as she slid a letter to her mother into an airmail envelope. Writing it had given her something to do, but without knowing how much her mother knew about Simpson's past, Gaelle daren't talk about Dan. Her letter sounded stilted as a result. She could only hope her mother wouldn't notice, being fully occupied with her new family in New Zealand.

She felt a pang of guilt, knowing she was neglecting her family and friends, but Dan filled her thoughts and her life until there was room for little esle.

Not for much longer, she thought unhappily. Once he found out the truth, he would go, and her life would return to its old tenor. The prospect filled her with despair.

But the knowledge couldn't stem the rush of gladness she felt as she heard the sound of his car pulling up outside. The throaty growl of his Jaguar Coupé was as distinctive as Dan's own voice, and sent the same thrill of recognition hurtling along her veins. She rushed to the window in time to see him climb out of the low-slung, copper-coloured car.

On the point of flinging open her front door, she stalled and took several deep breaths to quiet her racing heart. Dan wasn't a lover any more. He could be her brother, which was how she should greet him. She wiped moist palms down the sides of her slacks, then opened the door sedately.

'Good morning, Dan.' There, that was sisterly enough.

She had reckoned without her body's instinctive response to his nearness, and the heat which flooded her cheeks gave her away. His gaze travelled the length of her tailored navy slacks and lingered on her white lace-trimmed shirt, the pleated front rising and falling with her struggle to control her breathing. 'Hello, Gaelle.'

Abruptly she turned and led the way inside, before he could see how the mere use of her name inflamed her senses. This wasn't how she was suppsoe to react. Good grief, how was she to endure a day of this?

Dan didn't seem inclined to make things easier for her, and they drove the first few miles in strained silence. They were clear of the city, travelling south along the Hume Highway, when Gaelle felt she must break the silence or go crazy with unfulfilled longing. 'How did your business turn out yesterday?' she asked, hearing a tremor in her voice which she was powerless to control.

'Very well,' he said evenly. 'The sheikh thought I was stalling because I wanted a higher offer. He wants to pay me in money now, as well as oil wells and women.'

He named a figure that made her eyes widen. 'He must want you very badly!' she exclaimed.

Dan's mouth twisted into a wry grin, but he kept his gaze on the road ahead. 'More than some people, it seems.'

Gaelle ignored the taunt. 'Was that his wife with him?'

'One of them.'

The silence enfolded them again until it was a weight on her shoulders. She couldn't restrain the question any longer. She had to know. 'Are you going to go?'

The powerful car swerved fractionally before he brought it under control again. 'It would suit Guardino if I did, wouldn't it?'

She shot him a startled glance. 'Nick isn't in competition with you.'

'Oh, no? You could have fooled me, with all the hand-kissing and touching going on between you last night. What does Guardino do, anyway?'

The last thing she wanted to do was talk about Nick. His ghost had been well and truly exorcised last evening. 'He's a promoter of car racing, pop shows, that sort of thing,' she said in a low voice.

'And the glamour appeals to you, I suppose,' he

said derisively.

Pent-up tension made her temper flare and she twisted sideways until the bite of her seat-belt against her breasts brought her up short. 'Look, just because he doesn't take stupid risks with his life, it doesn't mean his work isn't important. He brings people a lot of pleasure.'

Dan ignored all but the first part of her outburst. 'So you believe that the risks I take are stupid, do you?'

It was too late to deny it now. 'Yes, I do. When I think of you dreaming up ways to outwit the world's terrorists, I go cold from head to foot. I just . . .' In horror, Gaelle let her voice die away, relising how completely she had betrayed herself to him.

'Go on,' he encouraged. 'This is so revealing.'

'What's wrong with caring what happens to a friend?' she demanded.

'Not a thing,' he said mildly. 'But Guardino is a friend, and you don't talk about him with that heart-rending catch in your voice, as if what happens to him happens to you, too.'

'You don't know what you're talking about,' said Gaelle as dismissively as she could.

Dan wasn't deceived for a minute. 'I believe I do. I think it's the key to your sudden change of heart. But you don't have to protect me. I can take care of myself.'

This time her confusion was genuine. 'I don't know what you mean.'

'You're trying to protect me with your heroic sacrifice. After all I said about not wanting to marry because of the risks, you're trying to let me off the hook by pretending to care about Guardino, aren't you?'

'No!' she protested. The idea had never entered her head.

He went on as if she hadn't spoken. 'There's no need to pretend any more, Gaelle. I was being foolish, cutting myself off from all ties because of the past. You made me see it. If you're willing to take a chance on me, the least I can do is meet you half-way. We very nearly didn't have any choice about it.'

It was the first time he'd referred to the baby. The thought of what they might have done filled her with horror. She turned pain-filled eyes to him. 'You don't understand,' she said.

'Yes, I do. Last night, you made me think you were in love with Guardino. I know it isn't true, because you don't talk about him the way you talk about me. If I wasn't already convinced, your response to me when we danced would have told me. You can hide your thoughts from me, but your body betrayed you with every step. Wasn't it why you left in such a hurry after our dance, because you knew your deception wasn't working?'

She'd left because she couldn't bear to stay with Nick, knowing her heart was with Dan. It wasn't fair to Nick. For once he had accepted her decision not to invite him in after he took her home. He seemed to sense the strength of her resolve. When he kissed her lightly, he said, 'I'm glad we finally had our farewell dinner. At least I know it's over. The best man won, and it wasn't me.'

Seeing her in Dan's arms, Nick must have drawn his own conclusions. Nick sounded so humble as he accepted the inevitable that Gaelle was touched. It was unlike him. She had kissed him back gently, but she knew when he walked away that she wouldn't see him again.

'Tell me, Gaelle, was this some crazy scheme to protect me?'

It was out before she could stop herself. 'Oh God, I wish it was!' she said fervently.

She was thrown sideways as the powerful car slewed to a halt on the grassy kerb. Cutting the engine, Dan turned to face her. 'Then what is it?' he demanded.

Her eyes blurred with tears, she shook her head. 'Can't you just accept that we're not right for each other, after all?'

He unsnapped his seat-belt and the small sound made her jump. 'If I accepted it, I wouldn't be here now. But I know you care, so there must be some other explanation for your sudden withdrawal.' He drew a long, shuddering breath. 'Was it something you found out about me? Something bad?'

Gaelle rested her forehead against the cool window glass, but he jerked her head around so she was forced to face him. 'Tell me.'

'No, I . . .'

'My God, it must be vile if you can't talk about it!' She flinched away from his hand. 'You can't even bear to have me touch you any more!' Suddenly he was shaking her so violently that her head began to ache. Sobs of despair racked her as he pulled her against him, disgust at his own actions written on his face. 'I'm sorry, Gaelle, so sorry.' His mouth clamped over hers, hungry and irresistible.

She had borne his violence without reaction, understanding how desperate he must feel. But the pressure on her mouth, and her body's instant craving for him, couldn't be countenanced. She struggled to free herself.

Dan grip tightened, but he freed her lips. 'I've got to know and you're going to tell me. What am I to you?'

The answer she could no longer withhold came out in an anguished cry. 'My brother!'

He flung her away as if she had confessed to murder. '*What* did you say?' he demanded.

Gaelle ached from his shaking, but ignored it and the painful jolt as her body collided with the car door. No pain could compare with Dan's suffering.

In a pain-filled whisper, she explained what she had learned about his past. 'I've been trying to find a way to tell you,' she finished. She turned her face away. 'Stop looking at me like that!'

'When did you find out?' he demanded. 'Dear lord, not before we . . .'

'No!' The protest was wrung from her. She couldn't let him think she had known when they made love. 'I didn't find out until a couple of days ago. That's why I've been staying away from you.'

His gaze was so unforgiving that it made her flinch. 'Exactly when did you plan on telling me?' he asked.

'When I was sure of my facts.' In a tremulous voice she explained about May Dreyfuss. 'She was a schoolfriend of my father's. I'm praying that she can tell us what really happened.'

'Surely a birth certificate is proof enough?'

'Only if the mother was telling the truth when

she filled in the details.

'And if she was?'

Dan knew the answer as well as she did, but she made herself spell it out. 'Then we're half-brother and sister, God help us!'

In the space of a few brief minutes Dan had changed from a teasing lover into a creature made of stone. This was painful for both of them, but he seemed impervious to Gaelle's suffering, having retreated into a mood so black, it frightened her.

She might as well have been alone in the car for all the response she got from him for the rest of the journey. He drove fast—faster than the speed limit, she was sure—but with iron control. Several times her heart was in her mouth as he overtook long lines of cars, but he always brought them back to their own side seconds ahead of the oncoming traffic. 'Dan, say something!' she pleaded after an hour of this.

'Say what?' he demanded. After the long silence, his booming demand startled her. 'Say I love you? I can't live without you? Or say I'm sorry? They all fit.'

'I know. But it wasn't our fault.'

The silence closed around them again. Afraid of provoking another useless outburst, Gaelle closed her eyes and tried to sleep. Her eyes had barely closed, it seemed to her, when the car slowed. The change in motion alerted her. They were entering Bundanoon.

Oaks and golden poplars lined the lanes of the township as the grassy slopes of the surrounding farm gave way to homesteads, churches and a cluster of shops. Sitting up, she gave Dan directions to May Dreyfuss's cottage, which was loacated just off the Highland Way.

'I thought you'd never been here,' Dan said gruffly.

'I haven't. But I came through here with Dad once and he pointed out the way to me.'

'Why didn't you visit her then?'

'Maybe she was away. How should I know?'

He gave her a curious glance, but said nothing. When they reached the address Gaelle had for May, she said, 'Do you mind if I go in alone? She may not want to talk about the past, but I'll have a better chance of persuading her on my own.'

He steered the car to a halt. 'I'll be back here at three to pick you up.'

In the act of getting out, she paused. 'What will you do in the meantime?' she asked.

'I'll go for a drive. I have a lot of thinking to do.'

A lump rose in her throat as she watched him drive away. He was acting as if the whole thing was her fault, when she was as much a victim as he was. She hadn't misled him deliberately, as he had half implied. He was shocked by her discovery, but it was no reason to take it out on her. If only he would talk to her, share his pain with her, she could help him through it.

No, she couldn't, she contradicted herself. If Dan unbent towards her, they both knew what would happen, and this time they wouldn't have the excuse of innocence. She looked after him in wonder. It wasn't anger he was directing at her, but a painfully built wall of indifference which they breached at their peril.

Dispiritedly Gaelle trudged up the flagstone path and knocked on May Dreyfuss's front door. At first she opened it warily, then she brightened when she recognised her caller. 'Gaelle Maxwell! This is a surprise.'

'I'm sorry to arrive unannouced, Mrs Dreyfuss. I know I should have telephoned . . .'

May cut her short. 'It's all right. What do you want?'

Gaelle shifted awkwardly from one foot to the other. 'Would you mind if I came in for a moment?'

'Well, I was planning to go out.'

Afraid that the door would be shut in her face, Gaelle plunged ahead. 'I need some information for a family history I'm writing. Since you went to school with my father, I thought you might be able to give me some background information.'

A change came over May. The wariness drained from her face and she broke into a welcoming smile. 'If that's all I'll be delighted to help.'

Perplexed by the change, Gaelle followed May down a corridor that ran the width of the weatherboard cottage. On both sides she glimpsed rooms filled with oversized furniture and bric-à-brac. The day was bright outside, but little sunlight pierced the layers of curtains that swathed the windows.

It was a relief to emerge into the kitchen where the sunlight streamed in unhindered. May gestured to some vinyl-covered chairs around a formica-topped table. 'Make yourself at home,' she invited.

'You must have thought I was selling something,' Gaelle said conversationally as she sat down.

May busied herself filling an earthenware teapot and putting fruit cake on to a plate. 'I didn't mean to sound brusque. You caught me off guard,' she explained.

Since May had recognised Gaelle on sight, the explanation seemed odd, but Gaelle pushed it aside. For all she knew, May could be the suspicious type who jumped at her own shadow. 'I'm glad you could spare me a few minutes,' she said warmly.

May placed tea and cake in front of her. 'I don't know how helpful I can be to you.'

'I mainly need details about Dad's teenage years. What life was like in his home town then, how he and his friends entertained themselves, that kind of thing. I meant to ask him myself, but . . .' Gaelle's voice faltered.

May patted her hand. 'I understand, dear. Nobody knew he had a weak heart. He showed no signs of it as a boy, always rushing around doing a million things at once.'

At the apt description of her father, Gaelle smiled. 'There were never enough hours in the day for him.'

The ice broken, May's face became wreathed in smiles. 'I know. But it paid off in the end. I heard he'd been made a professor at that university of his.'

'Not quite professor,' Gaelle admitted. 'He was a senior lecturer, though, and would have been made a full professor soon.'

'He'd have liked being called Professor,' May observed. 'He always was the studious type, and literature was his best subject all through high school.'

'So he didn't have much time for dating,' Gaelle hazarded.

May laughed. 'Far from it! He was very popular and good-looking, too. But you know that already.

I never knew how he fitted in so much study with his hectic social life, but he managed it somehow.'

'He never talked about those years,' said Gaelle. 'Was there a special girl in his life?'

'I suppose he didn't want to upset your mother, but there was someone very special.' May took a drink of tea. 'You can't need that for your history, though, and Simpson met your mother in Sydney, so I'm no help there.'

'I've heard how they met over a lunch counter at Coles' Cafeteria,' Gaelle explained. 'But I hadn't heard of a girlfriend before my mother. It's hard to imagine Dad being in love with anyone but Mum.'

'Oh, but he was,' May insisted—then realised she had let Gaelle provoke her into saying more. She thought for a moment, then relented. 'You may as well know. It's ancient history now anyway, what with Simpson gone and Mary too.'

Gaelle couldn't hold back her excited query. 'Mary Taylor?'

May looked startled. 'You know about her?'

'A little. Tell me, was my dad in love with her?'

'They were very much in love.'

With heavy heart, Gaelle realised that May was going to confirm everything she had suspected about her father and Mary Taylor. 'What happened?' she forced herself to ask, although she already knew the answer.

Carried away by her memories, May seemed to have forgotten her initial reluctance and Gaelle's reason for being here. 'It was terribly sad,' she went on. 'Mary and Simpson had just announced their engagement in the local paper when she discovered that she was going blind. Her eyesight had always troubled her, but she was devastated when she found out what was wrong. Nothing could be done.'

No wonder her father hadn't wanted to talk about those days! 'What did they do?' Gaelle asked softly.

'I remember the night Simpson found out. He came to see me because he didn't know where to turn. Mary had given him back his ring, insisting that she didn't want to be a burden to him. He tried to refuse, but she was adamant. When he couldn't change her mind, he took off for Sydney and never returned.'

'What became of Mary?'

'She couldn't face going blind. They found her in the river a few months later. Everybody said it was an accident, that she went swimming and was unable to see to find her way back to shore, but we'll never know for certain.'

The silence stretched into minutes as Gaelle digested this information. She had never imagined such a tragic story.

'Did Mary travel to Sydney for treatment sometimes?' she asked after a while.

May seemed to pull herself back to the present with an effort. 'Yes, I believe so,' she said. 'Why do you ask?'

Gaelle's thoughts raced. 'I was wondering if we ever met,' she said at last.

'I doubt it, she died before you were born,' May assured her.

The weight of Gaelle's new knowledge felt crushing. Dan's real mother was dead. Mary must have known she was pregnant when she sent

Gaelle's father away. Remembering Simpson Maxwell's fierce sense of honour, Gaelle knew he would never have left Mary otherwise. She felt a sudden pang for the girl, pregnant and alone, knowing she would soon be blind. Was that why she had abandoned her baby?

Unable to stem her sudden rush of tears, Gaelle bent her head and wept. She wasn't sure whether she was crying for Mary, Dan or herself. Perhaps all three of them, for they were bound together by a web of tragedy which still spun sadness so many years later.

'You poor child!' May went down on her knees beside Gaelle's chair and enfolded her in a comforting embrace. 'Was it Mary's story that upset you?'

Gaelle nodded and mopped futilely at her streaming eyes. May offered her a huge linen handkerchief and she buried her face in it. 'Thank you,' she sniffed.

'Surely this isn't all for Mary?' May asked.

Her voice was so soft and motherly, and her manner so undemanding, that Gaelle found herself spilling out the tale of her own lost baby. May kept her arms around her while she talked, and made no comments, only uttering soothing sounds of commiseration. At last Gaelle lifted her head. 'I feel such a fool, carrying on like this. What must you think of me?'

'Hush now, I don't think anything,' May chided gently. 'You don't get over such a loss easily, if you ever do. Give yourself time to heal.'

'You sound as if you know what it's like,' Gaelle

said wonderingly.

May bit her lip as if she was about to cry herself. 'I do, child, I do. Now come, drink your tea. You'll feel better for it.'

Sipping the hot liquid, Gaelle began to feel calmer. The mood between her and May had changed from that of polite strangers to close friends. Suddenly Gaelle understood why her father had valued May's friendship. You felt as if you could talk to her about anything. Gradually Gaelle found herself telling May about the baby Mary Taylor had given birth to in Sydney, then abandoned. 'She must have felt she couldn't care for it once her sight was gone,' she finished.

May gathered their cups and put them in the sink, keeping her back to Gaelle as she spoke. 'All the same, you mustn't be upset because you found out about Mary and your father.'

Suddenly Gaelle understood. May thought she was shocked by the discovery of her father's past. 'It isn't that,' she said hastily. 'I understand how Dad must have felt, so I don't hold any of it against him. But . . . oh God, how can I say it aloud?'

'Sometimes it's best just to say it,' May prompted.

Gaelle drew a shuddering breath. 'Recently, I fell in love with the most wonderful man in the world, the father of the child I lost. Then I found out that he was Mary Taylor's long-lost son.'

With a clatter, the cup dropped from May's hands, but she let it roll unheeded across the draining board. 'My lord! Does he know?'

'Yes.' Gaelle's tears welled up again and she dashed them away as she looked at May with tragic eyes. 'Oh, May, I I-love him so m-much, and now I have to give him up because our love is wrong. What am I going to do?'

May's own eyes were bright with tears as she rejoined Gaelle at the table. 'Don't, don't,' she crooned. 'I agree, it's a terrible, terrible discovery to make, but you'll learn to live without him.'

'I know. But it's killing me.'

May took both her hands and leaned closer. 'Surely love isn't everything? You'll still have him for a brother.'

Vehemently, Gaelle shook her head. 'No, I won't. He'll go away. Dan was afraid something like this would happen, so he never trusted himself to love anyone. I convinced him it was all right. He'll never take such a chance again.'

'Dan—is that his name?'

At the softness in May's voice, Gaelle lifted her head. 'Yes—Dan Buckhorn. He was fostered by the Lawson family. His foster-brother is Scott Lawson, the radio interviewer.'

'So he had a good life?'

'I suppose so.' Gaelle guessed that May was drawing her out to give her a chance to compose herself. She smiled gratefully. 'I'll be all right now.'

May returned her watery smile. 'Don't feel badly about letting go. We all need to sometimes.'

'All the same, it wasn't why I came,' Gaelle said self-deprecatingly.

'I'm sure Simpson would want me to help his daughter,' May assured her. 'I just wish there was something more I could do for you.'

'You've been kindness itself.' Gaelle glanced at her

watch, appalled to find that her time was almost up. 'I must go. I'm being picked up shortly.'

There was a softness around May's features that hadn't been there when Gaelle arrived. She smiled. 'By Dan?'

'Yes. I'll bring him in if you like. After all this, I should introduce you to him.'

'No, don't do that!' May's sharp response startled Gaelle but she added quickly, 'I have an appointment to go to.'

'Of course—you said you were going out. I'm sorry for keeping you.'

The emotionally charged atmosphere of the last few minutes had evaporated, leaving them back where they started. 'Not at all, Gaelle. I hope you'll come and see me again.'

Even as she agreed that she would, Gaelle knew she was unlikely to return. The town held too much sadness for her. She told herself she would write to May instead, but wondered if this too was a brave lie.

There was no sign of Dan's car when Gaelle reached the kerb. She looked over her shoulder, expecting to see May come out of the house on the way to her appointment, but she didn't emerge. Anxiously, Gaelle scanned both approaches to the house.

She had just began to worry when she heard the distant growl of the jaguar, then it crested the rise and crunched to a stop on the gravel verge, churning dust around it. Dan leaned across and opened the passenger door for her. 'Ready to go?'

Averting her tear-stained face, she nodded.

When she kept silent, his fingers drummed against

the steering wheel. 'Well? Is it true?'

'Yes, it's true. Mary Taylor and my father were enaged to be married, but she broke it off when she found out she was losing her sight.'

He sucked in his breath. 'So she's blind. Where is she now?'

Her hand went to his arm. 'Dan, I'm so sorry. She drowned soon after you were born.'

He looked at her hand for a long time, then carefully lifted it and returned it to her lap. 'I see. Then there's no doubt?'

'Apparently not. Mrs Dreyfuss said the engagement was announced in the local paper. I could look it up.'

Dan slammed his hands against the steering wheel. 'What good would that do?'

'I guess I was hoping . . .'

'Well, stop hoping. It's over.'

Would it ever be over? Gaelle asked herself despairingly. Would she ever forget what they had been to each other and learn to think of Dan as a brother? 'What are you going to do?' she asked fearfully.

'What I must. Take up the Middle East assignment and all the ones that come after it.'

'You won't come back to Australia?'

His gaze swung to her, as if he was drinking in a last sight of her to sustain him in the years ahead. 'I couldn't trust myself. God, Gaelle, how can I, when every second we're together, I want to hold you and never let you go? I'd almost prefer it if you *did* love Nick. I could fight him. I can't fight this. I have to go.'

'But you're my brother,' she choked on the word, knowing the heartache it encompassed. 'We're family!'

His eyes were dark with anguish. 'Which is precisely why I daren't stay around you. I told you not to love me, you should have listened.'

'But it was innocent. We didn't know.'

'However innocent, it's still wrong. Since I can't change the way I feel about you, I'm going to get the hell out of your life while I still can.'

He was right. Still, Gaelle looked wildly around, as if some reason would appear for him to stay. May's house met her gaze, but there was no help there. As she looked, a curtain dropped into place across the window and her confused mind registered the fact that May had been watching them. Gaelle could feel the woman's eyes on them as they drove away.

CHAPTER TEN

GAELLE hadn't heard from Dan in over a week. He was probably half-way across the world by now, sorting out the security problems of his Middle Eastern sheikh. Still she couldn't rid herself of the hope that flared inside her every time the phone rang.

It couldn't be him ever again, she chided herself when it happened for the fourth time that morning. Even if he called, what could they say to each other that hadn't been said on the way home from Bundanoon?

The journey had been agony as every mile brought them closer to the inevitable parting. She had been sure she would break down, but her tears must have spent themselves at May's house. But the time Dan pulled up outside Gaelle's terrace house in Clontarf, she had no tears left. She felt empty inside, as if all the life had been drained from her body.

When he came around to her side of the car and opened he door, she emerged stiff-legged and cold, like a puppet. 'This is goodbye, then?'

'It has to be,' he reminded her. 'Don't make it any harder than it is, for both our sakes.'

How could she make it harder when it already cost her every ounce of strength she possessed just to take a step away from him inside her own gate? 'You're not coming in?'

'I shouldn't.' Still, he had sounded as reluctant as she did.

'Just for a minute,' she begged. 'I want to say goodbye properly, not out here in the street.'

'Just for a minute, then.'

Gaelle wasn't sure what she meant by a proper goodbye. The one her heart ached for was forbidden to them, and a sisterly peck on Dan's cheek would only kindle flames which were better being allowed to die out. The embers of their love, she thought. It was too poetic a description for such a bleak reality.

He had solved the problem by sitting down on her couch, keeping the breadth of the coffee table between them. 'It hurts, doesn't it?' he said.

'Yes.'

'Are you sorry you persisted with your research?'

She looked down at her hands, inspecting each fingernail as if they fascinated her. 'No. I'm glad you know who you are and where you come from. At least I could give you that.'

'You've given me a great deal more, Gaelle.' Dan's voice reached her as a gruff undertone. 'I never let myself love before.'

Hysterical laughter bubbled out of her throat. 'Look where it got you!'

'Stop it,' he commanded fiercely. 'I know what we did was totally wrong, but I can't make myself regret it. I want you to know, Gaelle, I love you and I always will.'

The tears she'd thought were finished blurred her vision as she looked up at him, her hands gripping the edge of the table. 'I love you too.'

'I know.' She noticed that his knuckles were also white against the table edge and his whole body angled forward, as if he unconsciously strained to reach her. His eyes locked with hers, their iridescence at once challenging and inviting. Suddenly he said, 'I'm kissing you now. Can you feel it?'

Her tongue darted across her top lip. 'Yes—oh yes, yes!'

'Now my arms are around you. Can you feel that?'

Miraculously, the warmth of them enfolded her and she nodded. 'I feel them.'

'Now your head is on my shoulder and your weight is braced against me. There, is it good?'

Her slight body shudderred as her imagination supplied the hardness of his physique aligned with hers. She half rose, but Dan motioned her back. 'Stay there. Just feel what I tell you to feel.'

Obediently she had closed her eyes, and travelled with him on a journey of the imagination, to heights of sensation she had never dreamed were possible. Perhaps in reality they would still be impossible, happening only in the realm of the mind.

Just remembering the experience made her feel loose-jointed and weak, her nerve-endings throbbing as if he had actually touched her. They had not kissed in parting, but at her door, Dan had described his kiss in such vivid word-pictures that her mouth felt swollen and bruised, as if he had really kissed her. Her hand strayed to her mouth as she remembered the scene. Neither of them had wanted to say the inal words, but Dan had somehow mustered the strength. 'Take care, my heart,' he had said, and walked away.

He hadn't looked back. Gaelle was glad, because he didn't want his parting view of her to be clouded by tears. She gave vent to those much later, only alling into a restless sleep in the small hours of the norning.

Now, a week later, peace of mind still eluded her. Outwardly, her life went on as usual. She nterviewed her clients and spent hours at the library, drugging her mind with research until she came home so tired that she could barely see. But inwardly, he felt frozen, as if a layer of ice covered her emotions.

The phone rang again, and this time she cut off the rush of anticipation before it fully began. 'Gaelle Maxwell,' she answered in clipped tones.

'Ah, Gaelle, this is Scott Lawson. How are you?'

Scott Lawson, Dan's foster-brother. At the sound of his voice, an echo of Dan's, the longing began again. It was an effort to answer him normally. 'I'm ine, thank you. What can I do for you?'

'Firstly, I owe you an apology for not helping you ocate Dan last time you came on my show.'

'He explained the problem. There's no need to pologise, I understand why you couldn't tell ne.'

'Nevertheless, I gave you a hard time and I'm orry. No hard feelings?'

'Of course not,' Gaelle agreed. 'It's all over, orgotten.' Like a lot of things, she added to herself.

'It was nice of you to call and tell me.'

He chuckled, sounding so like Dan that her heart muscles constricted in protest. 'Actually, it was more selfish than nice. I was hoping you would agree to come on the show again. We got a lot of mail about your segment. People have written in asking how they can find adopted children, convict ancestors and living relatives. I'm swamped!'

In spite of the reasons why she should refuse, Gaelle wavered. 'I can help you deal with the mail,' she offered, 'but I was sick with nerves last time, so I don't know about coming on the show.'

'You were a beginner,' he coaxed. 'This time it will be much easier. You're a veteran performer now. Say you'll do it!'

'It's easy to see why you get interviews nobody else can,' she said with grudging admiration. Despite the butterflies which were already gathering in her stomach, she was tempted. Having had the same upbringing, Scott reminded her so much of Dan that it was like being near him again. It was the wrong reason to agree, but she found herself saying yes as if another part of her had taken over.

'I'm delighted,' Scott enthused. 'Wait until I tell Dan you're coming in!'

Gaelle's throat tightened and she swallowed convulsively. 'Is he still in Sydney?' she asked.

'Until his Persian Gulf thing gets underway,' Scott told her. 'I hoped you two might make a match of it, and make my life simpler.'

'In what way?' she asked, puzzled.

He laughed. 'If you were a memeber of the family, I could use my influence to have you on the show as a regular.'

If he only knew, she was already practically a member of his family. It might have been an asset to Scott, but Gaelle would have given everything she owned to change matters. 'Dan and I are just friends,' she told Scott.

'Pity. But I can understand you not wanting to tie yourself to a man who spends half his life hanging around airports, and the other half playing Sky Marshal while he makes sure his security systems work. It must be worse than being married to a radio journalist.'

Since she would never know what marriage to Dan would be like, Gaelle made no comment. She let Scott settle the arrangements for her second appearance on his show, then hung up.

What a fool she was! Now she had committed herself to making a broadcast that scared her silly, and all because Scott reminded her of Dan. She wished he hadn't told her that Dan was still in the country. The thought that he was only a few suburbs away made her want to jump into the car and go to him.

This was hopeless. Switching off her computer, she reached for her handbag. A mountain of research awaited her at the State Library. At least there she would be too busy to think about Dan.

She was wrong. Even among towering stacks of books, he haunted her. As she walked past the entrance to the newspaper files, she felt a tug. Surely it wouldn't hurt to look up the Bundanoon newspapers?

Dan was probably right, it wouldn't change anything. But it would give her an insight into her father's character which she needed now. After learning about his engagement to Mary Taylor, Gaelle felt as if she hadn't really known him at all.

Before she realised what she was doing, her feet had taken her into the newspaper room. A voice she hardly recognised as her own asked the librarian for the papers she needed. Since she knew the approximate date when her father had arrived in Sydney, she soon worked out which newspapers to request, allowing a few weeks either side as a margin for error.

Less than an hour later the picture lay in front of her, and she studied it in fascination. So this was Mary Taylor! Dan's mother, she thought with a rush of emotion. She was a beautiful woman.

According to the caption, both she and Simpson were nineteen when the picture was taken. Even the large owl-glasses couldn't dim Mary's fragile beauty. Tall and willowy, she clung to Simpson's arm and his hand covered hers in a gesture of reassurance. Gaelle smiled involuntarily. They looked like a couple in love.

Her father had been a handsome man, she realised. He had always been good-looking, but in his youth it was easy to see why he never lacked for dates. Idly she traced a finger over the picture, wishing it could tell her the secret of Mary Taylor's attraction. Was it the serenity which she radiated? Gaelle's father had prized independence in everyone, male and female, so Mary's clinging-vine looks must have been deceptive.

She had been strong enough to bear a child alone and in secret, far away from her family and friends, Gaelle reminded herself. If her death wasn't an accident, what strength of mind was required to make such a decision? To her surprise, Gaelle looked up from the old newspaper to find that her cheeks were wet.

While she composed herself, she turned the pages of the newspaper, gaining a picture of life in the Southern Highland town when her father was a boy. The headlines ranged over debates about local highways to the threatened closure of a nearby cinema. The sports pages dwelt on the exploits of the cricket team while the social pages announced engagements and marriages, birth and deaths as they still did today.

An item about the Sydney Royal Easter Show caught her eye and she began to read it. Apparently some local residents had gained awards in various catagories. Among those being congratulated was Mary Taylor, whose handmade lace took first prize for handicrafts. Thinking of her skill in trimming the baby dress, Gaelle thought the award was well deserved. She was sorry there were no pictures of the winners or their work; she would have liked to see the lace which won Mary her prize.

With a start, Gaelle realised she had spent much too long in the newspaper section. Feeling guilty, she took the paper to a librarian and showed him the engagement picture. 'Would you copy this for me?' she asked.

The man glanced at it. 'Is Bundanoon having an

anniversary or something?'

'I don't know. Why?'

'You're the second person I've copied that page for this week.'

Telling herself it must be coincidence, Gaelle paid for the photocopy and went into the main library to continue her delayed research project. By the time she had finished, the puzzle had slipped from her mind.

It wasn't until the next morning that she remembered it. She was on her way to Scott's studio after delivering the outline of a family history to a client, when it came back to her. The only person who could have asked for the photocopy was Dan himself. In spite of what he'd said, was he still hoping to find out something new?

Her heart ached with love for him. Until yesterday she had wanted the same thing. Now, it seemed hopeless.

If May's testimony and the engagement picture weren't enough, the snippet about Mary Taylor's prize for lacemaking provided the final indictment.

But did it? Shocked by what she was thinking, Gaelle almost drove her car into a telephone pole before wrestling it back under control. Why hadn't she thought of it before? She fought her rising excitement, telling herself that she could be wrong, but she had to find out for sure.

Jill's surgery was only a few blocks from her, so she drove straight there. Jill's morning surgery should be over by now. With luck, she would catch the doctor before she went to lunch.

Her luck held and Jill looked up, smiling, as Gaelle was shown into her office. Then she frowned. 'Nothing's wrong, I trust?'

'I'm feeling fine, honestly,' Gaelle hastened to reassure her. 'But there was something I needed to ask about.'

Jill kicked off her shoes and swung her feet on to her desk. 'Ask away.'

Haltingly, Gaelle described the symptoms suffered by Mary Taylor as May Dreyfuss had relayed them to her. 'What does it sound like to you?' she asked when she finished.

Jill shrugged. 'It could be a number of things, mostly treatable now, but probably not at the time you describe. For instance, she could have glaucoma or various diseases of the retina, all leading to eventual blindness.'

Curbing her excitement, Gaelle seized on the word. 'By eventual, you mean it happened gradually?'

'Most likely. Sudden blindness is more commonly associated with an accident. Why do you ask?'

'I need to know whether someone suffering from one of these diseases could do fine needlework?'

Emphatically, Jill shook her head. 'Glasses would have helped some conditons, but there would always be some degree of impairment, especially when the condition was as advanced as you describe,'

Gaelle jumped up, 'I could hug you, Doctor Jill!'

To the doctor's surprise, she did just that. Jill laughed. 'I wish you'd tell me what I did!'

'You solved a mystery for me. I'll tell you all about it one day.'

'Along with all the others you've promised to explain,' Jill said drily. 'I should be on your staff, with the amount of information I supply.'

'I'll pay you in lace,' Gaelle promised her. 'I've nearly finished edging your tablecloth.'

'In that case, you're forgiven!'

With a much lighter heart, Gaelle drove to the radio station where Scott Lawson was expecting her. He was on the air when she arrived, but his researcher, Helen Otford, greeted Gaelle like an old friend. Fortunately, she seemed to have forgotten Gaelle's contrived clumsiness last time they had met.

'It's good to have you on the show again,' she enthused. 'I hope you're feeling more confident this time.'

Buoyed up by what she had learned about Mary Taylor, Gaelle had almost forgotten to be nervous at all. She only wanted the interview to be over so she could continue her enquiries.

After a short wait, she was shown into the studio from which Scott was broadcasting. As she was fitted with headphones, he gave her the thumbs-up sign. She smiled back, only now feeling apprehensive. It would be soon over, she told herself, then she could pursue the mystery that stood between her and Dan.

Preoccupied, she had to school herself to pay attention as listeners rang in with their questions about genealogy. The open-line programme needed all her concentration as she answered the questions which were thrown at her.

At last Scott looked at the massive studio clock. 'We've time for one more caller before we take a news break,' he said in to the microphone.

The line crackled for a moment, then erupted with the sound of a woman sobbing. 'I need to know how to find my child,' she gasped through her tears.

'You mean, you gave him up for adoption?' Gaelle asked, darting an alarmed look at Scott. He frowned, but gestured for her to continue.

'No, I left him outside a children's home,' the woman went on, her distress mounting. 'I was desperate, but I've regretted that moment all my life. Now I want to know how to find him again.'

For a confused moment Gaelle wondered if it was Dan's mother calling, then she pulled herself together. Other children had been abandoned by distraught mothers. All the same, as she heard the panic in the woman's voice, she understood how Mary Taylor must have felt, walking away from her child, never to know what happened to it. There was a tremor in Gaelle's voice as she described the steps the woman could take to try to trace her son. 'I don't know if any of them will work, but it's all I can suggest,' she concluded.

There was a loud sniff. 'Thank you and God bless you, Miss Maxwell,' the caller said, heartfelt.

At Scott's signal, a commercial began to play and he motioned her to remove her headphones. 'That call really got to you, didn't it?' he asked.

Gaelle blinked the mist from her eyes. 'I don't

know why it should,' she told him.

He regarded her keenly. 'It wouldn't have anything to do with Dan? I gather he told you about his background.'

'Listening to that poor woman, I couldn't help thinking of his real mother,' she confessed.

He removed his glasses and massaged his eyes. 'I know what you mean.' Suddenly he looked up. 'You know he cares about you?'

Dumbly she nodded, still too affected by the caller to trust her voice.

'Yet you're willing to let him go without a fight? I got a different impression of you last time, somehow.'

His goad went home and her head came up. 'You're right—I am a fighter. But sometimes you're defeated before you start.'

His curiosity was piqued, she could see from the intent way he looked at her. But the technician called his attention to the end of the break. 'I have to go on to my next guest,' he said apologetically. 'Helen will take you to my office and let you look through some of the mail. The station will pay you for your time of course.'

Gaelle waved his suggestion away. 'There's no need, I'm glad to be of help.' But Scott was already turning back to his microphone, and he waved his goodbye as Helen showed her out of the studio.

'You were terrific,' she said when they were outside the double-thickness doors of the studio. 'What about that woman who abandoned her baby? How could she do such a thing?'

'We don't know anything about her circumstances.

Maybe she had no choice,' Gaelle said more sharply than she intended.

Startled, Helen held up her hands. 'I didn't mean to upset you!'

Evidently she didn't know the story of Dan's background, Gaelle realised. She smiled at the researcher. 'It's all right. I guess I'm still keyed up after the interview.'

'It's OK—I understand.'

Helen made no more disparaging remarks as she took Gaelle to Scott's office and showed her the pile of mail. Gaelle skimmed through the letters. 'Most of these questions seem to be routine,' she said thankfully.

'If you write your suggestions on the bottom of each one, we'll have them typed up on studio letterhead,' Helen told her. She grinned. 'You could have yourself a regular job here, the way this is snowballing!'

'I don't know, said Gaelle. 'I couldn't handle too many emotional callers. I'd come unglued myself.'

'Wait till you have to keep a suicide talking while the police trace the call,' Helen told her. 'That's Scott's speciality. And speaking of whom . . .' She made her apologies, saying she would go back to the studio to be on hand in case Scott needed her.

Glad to be alone at last, Gaelle sat back in Scott's chair. The call about the abandoned baby had shaken her more than she had admitted to Scott or Helen. She hoped Dan hadn't heard the call. The woman had sounded so shattered, she had barely been able to talk. Was that how Mary Taylor had felt about

Dan? Gaelle wondered at the pressure she must have endured before she decided to walk away from her baby when every instinct called her back.

As emotion threatened to overwhelm her again, Gaelle reached for the first of the letters and made herself concentrate on answering them. The time flew and it was after lunch before she raised her head.

She told herself it must be tiredness making her see things. Dan was standing in the doorway, watching her at work. 'Hello, Gaelle,' he said softly.

She wasn't imagining him, after all. Containing the pleasure that surged through her, she returned his greeting. 'Scott told me you were still in Sydney. How are you?'

He shrugged. 'The same. It was Scott's idea to get me here today. He seems to think you can prevent me from leaving the country.'

'Maybe I can,' she murmured, thinking of what she had discovered before the interview.

His expression became pained. 'We've been over that, and it's for the best if I go.'

Gaelle leaned forward intently. 'Maybe not. I've been doing some more research.' She pulled out the engagement picture she'd carried in her handbag since yesterday.

Dan's glance flickered to the picture and back to her. 'I know. I found the pictures too.'

So he was the owner of the other photocopy! Forcing her voice to stay steady, she said, 'In that case, you know that Mary Taylor was half blind when the picture was taken.'

'So what? We already knew she was losing her sight.'

She went around the desk, stopping only feet away from him. 'But don't you see—in the same week, she also won first prize for her lacemaking at the Royal Easter Show!'

For a moment, a faint light stirred in his eyes, then he closed his lids, shuttering them. When he opened them to look at her, the light was gone. 'She probably made the stuff months before, when her eyes were still good.'

Violently, Gaelle shook her head. 'I spoke to Jill, and she says this kind of eye trouble deteriorates over years. She couldn't have made the lace at all.'

'You're clutching at straws,' he insisted. 'Without knowing exactly what was wrong with her eyesight, you can't be sure it wasn't something sudden.'

Longing for him exploded like a firecracker inside her. 'I have to clutch at straws! Scott's right—I can't let you walk out of here, out of my life!'

Before she had fully formulated the action, she went to him and linked her arms around his neck. She expected him to push her away, but his embrace enfolded her. With a thrust of his hand he pushed her head back and his mouth clamped hungrily over hers. His kiss was savage and demanding, but she gloried in it, giving as much as she took from him. She could feel the heat radiating from him, searing her through her clothes. Desperately, they clung together.

Tearing his mouth from hers, Dan flung her bodily back against the desk. She held on to it, feeling her legs tremble under her. His expression was bleak. 'Are you satisfied? This is what happens when we're in the same room together for five minutes. And you want me to stay?'

The cry came from her heart. 'I need you to stay. What if I'm right and Mrs Dreyfuss didn't tell us all she knows? Won't you even come to Bundanoon with me to find out?'

'I dare not. We both know where it would lead, and there's no excuse this time. I know as much as I need to already. My birth certificate has Mary Taylor's name on it, with Simpson Maxwell as my father. We've both seen their engagement announcement. Haven't we been through enough, for pity's sake?'

'No, not when our happiness depends on whether we can endure for just a little longer. I have to know, Dan! I couldn't bear the thought that I hadn't done all I could.'

With infinite gentleness he touched her cheek, then let his finger trail down her face, collecting a teardrop as he went. The tenderness of the gesture tore at her heartstrings. 'Believe me, darling, if there was anything we could do to change things, I would do it, for my sake as well as yours. Do you think it's easy for me to walk away from you? But if I learned anything in the Middle East it's to live with Fate. I change what I can and accept what I must.' His hand dropped to his side. 'You must, too. Find yourself a man you're free to love with all your heart. My God, I know what a pearl beyond price you are! I'd give my life to know it again, but it wouldn't change anything. Torturing yourself isn't the way.'

Gaelle's breathing was ragged as she lifted a tear-stained face to him. 'Then tell me what is?'

'Go on with your life. Forget me.'

'Is that what you're going to do? Forget me?'

Dan's bleak gaze raked her, then he closed his eyes as if in pain. When he spoke, his voice was low and vibrant with emotion. 'It would take a miracle for me to forget you. But we have to try.'

Frozen by the weight of all that stood between them, they stood like statues, longing to reach out, yet bound by society's conventions to stay apart. It was as if a wall stood between them, through which they could see but not touch each other. Dan was right, that was how it had to be.

'Oh, there you are—I've been looking all over!'

The spell binding them shattered as a statuesque blonde breezed into the room. Seeing Dan's intent expression, she halted. 'Am I interrupting something?'

'No, I was just coming,' Dan said harshly. 'Gaelle, this is Gloria Roanoak, she's an air hostess.'

The woman grimaced. 'They call us flight attendants these days, darling. Hi, Gaelle.' Before Gaelle could respond to the half-hearted greeting, Gloria turned to Dan. 'Your car is downstairs and I've made reservations at the Bennelong for dinner.'

Dan roused himself with an apparent effort. 'I'll be down in a few mintues. Wait for me in the car.'

A sulky look settled on Gloria's face and she seemed about to say something, then she saw Dan's look. 'I'll be downstairs,' she murmured and turned on her heel.

Gaelle felt as though her heart had been carved into little pieces and scattered on the wind. 'You're doing very well at forgetting,' she taunted, hurt making her bitter.

Dan gestured dismissively. 'She isn't you and never could be.'

'Is she going to the Persian Gulf?'

'Yes, Gloria fancies herself in a harem.'

So that was that. He wasn't even going to look any further for the truth that could give them a chance. Gaelle felt cold from head to foot as she said, 'Well, I'm glad you got your miracle after all.'

His words echoed between them, unspoken but vivid in both their minds—*it would take a miracle to make me forget you.* 'It isn't like that,' he said heavily. 'I'm just going on, as best I can.'

'Your best is startlingly successful!' She turned her head away so he wouldn't see the tears that brightened her eyes. Damn him! He might at least pretend he was sorry about what happened, instead of blithely replacing her and going on, as he put it.

His voice reached her from far away. 'One day you'll understand, Gaelle. Whatever you think, Gloria isn't my miracle. But I pray you find yours soon. It's all I can wish for you.'

Then he was gone, and Gaelle was alone, tormented by the awareness that he was on his way to his car to join the lovely Gloria. She should have been at his side, she told herself savagely. He had wished her a miracle. Couldn't he see that he was the only miracle she ever wanted? No man could satisfy her after him, no matter what stood between them.

Dan hadn't said when he was leaving for the Middle East. She hoped to goodness it wasn't too soon. Because, no matter what he said, she intended to make her own miracle. Her eyes went to the newspaper cutting still lying on Scott's desk. Everything depended on whether or not May Dreyfuss was telling the whole truth.

CHAPTER ELEVEN

IN FRUSTRATION, Gaelle slammed the telephone down. She had been trying to contact May Dreyfuss all morning, but the number rang and rang with no answer. The woman was entitled to go out for the day, Gaelle told herself, but it didn't stop her feeling desperate. The minutes were ticking by. Even now, Dan could be on his way to the Middle East. With Gloria, a traitorous inner voice whispered.

She crossed the study and picked up the tablecloth she was edging for Jill. Since she was unable to still her mind, perhaps it would help if her hands had something to do.

But even the steady looping and twisting of the shuttle and ball of thread didn't calm her. Despairingly, she looked at the butterfly pattern and saw that she had forgotten to finish one wing. She reached for her unpicker and began to undo her work, half-stitch by half-stitch. Then she set to work on the heart-shaped motifs again, this time getting them right. Leaving long ends to form into antennae which she would finish with Josephine knots, she set the work down. It was no good. She would have no peace until she spoke to Mrs Dreyfuss.

When another attempt yielded no answer, she decided that enough was enough. Krys had invited her to the opening of her new exhibition at the

Glenfield Gallery in Paddington. She hadn't planned to go, but now she had to get out of the house or go crazy with the strain of waiting.

Half an hour later, she had changed her jeans and T-shirt for a cobalt jersey dress with a becoming cowl neckline, teamed the dress with black patent leather accessories, and was on her way to Paddington.

The gallery was already thronged with people when she pulled up outside the main entrance of the Regency brick building, but she was lucky to find a parking space nearby. Krys's face lit up with pleasure when she saw Gaelle. 'I didn't think you were coming!' she said.

Feeling guilty because she had almost talked herself out of it, Gaelle flushed. 'I haven't been out much lately.'

'Who is he?' Krys demanded excitedly.

'Why does it have to be a man? I could have been working,' Gaelle defended herself.

Krys grinned. 'Work never gave you that gleam in your eye!' She looked knowing. 'I'll bet it's the mystery man from the murder weekend.'

'Well, I have been seeing him,' Gaelle dissembled.

Mercilessly, Krys pounced. 'I knew it! You were much too interested in him for a casual enquiry. Who was he in the end?'

'You were right,' Gaelle admitted reluctantly. 'It was Scott Lawson's guest, Dan Buckhorn. There was no mystery, really. He was just entering into the spirit of the weekend.'

'I'm glad. I didn't like the idea of a strange man crashing one of my parties.'

'Well, now you can stop worrying—and stop tormenting me.'

'Would I do that, Gaelle?' All right, I would, but it must be serious. I haven't seen you in days.'

Gaelle had come here to get away from thoughts of Dan, not to discuss him endlessly with Krys. 'I'm here now, so show me some pictures I can't afford,' she urged.'

Successfully diverted, Krys took her on a tour of the latest Doyle offerings. They were all in black and white line, which had become Krys's trademark. As Gaelle suspected, the prices were all breathtakingly high. Generously, Krys offered to make her a present of anything that took her fancy. 'For your birthday, she insisted.

'But my birthday is months away,' Gaelle protested. She was saved the embarrassment of having the gift thrust upon her when a journalist arrived to interview Krys. 'Duty calls—see you in a while,' the artist said, and sailed off.

Feeling relieved, Gaelle watched her go. Krys was like a hunter on the scent of her prey. Once she got an idea into her head, she wouldn't let it rest until she had exhausted it. There was no way Gaelle could keep her feelings for Dan a secret from Krys for long. And she couldn't face any more well-meaning questions about him right now.

Her gaze roved over the crowd of art-lovers and members of the media, until she realised that the profile she had been unconsciously seeking wasn't there. Her eyes rested on a tall, broad-shouldered man with short-cropped dark hair for a moment, then her heart stopped. But it was only Scott Lawson, she

saw when he turned. He saw her and made his way
through the crowd towards her, lifting two glasses of
champagne off the waiter's tray as he came.

They exchanged greetings and he handed her one
of the glasses. 'I've been meaning to thank you for
helping with the mail,' he said.

Gaelle sipped the effervescent liquid. 'I was glad to
do it. Once I got over my nerves, I enjoyed being on
your show.'

'Didn't I tell you so?' he said with the air of one
who is usually right. 'Dan thinks you should host a
regular family history segment.'

It was out before she could prevent it. 'Is he still in
Sydney?'

His eyebrow arched. 'I don't know. The last I
heard, his sheikh had put a time limit on his job offer.
It's due to expire at midnight tomorrow, so Dan has
to be on the plane by then or the offer lapses. He
doesn't have much reason to stay, does he?' He
watched her over the rim of his glass.

Miserably, she shook her head. 'I suppose
not.'

He lowered his head so it was close to hers. 'You
aren't letting his background stand in your way, are
you?'

How could he think she was so shallow? 'I'm not
that big a fool!' she retorted.

'Then why . . .'

'It's a long story, Scott,' Gaelle interrupted him.
Evidently Dan hadn't shared their recent discovery
with his foster-family.

'In other words, mind your own business, Scott.'

'I didn't mean it that way——' she began.

'Yes, you did, and you're quite right. I guess I got into the habit of defending Dan when he was small. I occasionally forget that he hasn't needed protecting since he was ten years old. He's pretty special, our Dan.'

Too overcome by emotion to speak, Gaelle nodded and took a long sip of her champagne. It seemed as if everywhere she turned the aura of Dan surrounded her. Even here, she was unable to escape his influence. Frantically she thought of something to say to change the subject, but her mind was blank.

She was saved when Scott spotted an acquaintance across the room and waved. 'I'll introduce you to Alex Porter, the film producer,' he offered.

With her luck he would turn out to be another of Dan's admirers, Gaelle thought, growing desperate. 'I'm sorry, I have to go,' she apologised. 'I only stopped by for a short visit.'

Scott accepted her excuse with good grace and went to join his friend. Before anyone else could waylay her, she sought out Krys and gave her the same excuse.

Krys was less easily convinced. 'Are you sure you're all right? You look pale. Love is supposed to make you bloom.'

'I'm not pale and I'm not in love,' Gaelle assured her, putting as much conviction as she could into her voice. 'I'll call you.'

Squeezing her friend's hand in farewell, she turned and fled before Krys could ask any more awkward questions.

As she sat in her car, alone at last, her eyes went to

her reflection in the driving mirror. Krys was right: she was pale and she was in love. And knowing that Dan was probably getting ready to leave the country right now didn't help a bit.

There was still no answer from May Dreyfuss when Gaelle tried her number again at home. She let it ring for a long time before replacing the receiver. This was useless. She couldn't work, she couldn't sew, and, as she'd just proved, she couldn't socialise properly while every nerve in her body was vibrant with longing for Dan. May Dreyfuss was the only person who could make things right between them.

Gaelle looked at the clock. It was already early afternoon. She had to talk to May before Dan got on his plane tomorrow. There was only one way.

In less time than it had taken her to get ready for Kry's opening, she had changed back into her jeans, packed an overnight bag and was in her car, heading south. 'Please don't let her be away,' she prayed as she negotiated the busy traffic clogging the city fringes. Soon she was out in the countryside, the Hume Highway unfolding under her wheels.

How different this trip was from the one she had taken with Dan! Then, he'd been the driver, and she had been free to admire the casual way he handled his powerful car, his long-fingered hands resting lightly on the wheel as his gaze flickered from the road to her and back again. She could almost feel the warmth of his caressing gaze on her. What was he doing now? Were his thoughts dominated by her, as hers were by him? Or had he truly managed to go on, with the lovely Gloria for company? Remembering the possessive way the statuesque air hostess had behaved towards him, Gaelle gritted her teeth. Maybe she was too late, and this trip was a waste of time.

She didn't know what she expected to find. As Dan had said, the evidence of the birth certificate and the engagement photo was almost overwhelming. If Gaelle had been researching for a client, she would have accepted them as positive proof of Dan's background. Was she quibbling only because she wanted things to be different; clutching at straws, as Dan put it? Yes, she admitted. But there was more. Her researcher's instinct couldn't accept the conflict between Mary Taylor's failing sight and the exquisite lace she had supposedly made. Gaelle knew she wouldn't rest until she knew the answers.

It was late by the time she approached the township. The shadows were lengthening over the grassy slopes and rugged mountain ranges cradling Bundanoon. Every instinct urged her to drive straight to May Dreyfuss's house, but she hesitated. If what she had begun to suspect was true, she wanted the moment to be right when she approached May. It cost her emotionally, but she made herself drive past May's turn-off and pull up outside the Boronia Motel in Anzac Parade where a 'vacancy' sign flashed behind a screen of tall pines.

The owner was a grandmotherly type who showed Gaelle to her room, then lingered to point out the best craft shops in the area. 'You can hire a bicycle if you want to cycle through the National Park,' she said helpfully. It was easier to let the woman believe Gaelle was here to relax, so she murmured her thanks.

To her surprise, she slept well that night and awoke refreshed as sunlight streamed into her room. For a moment she couldn't think where she was, then memory came flooding back. She sat up with a jolt. If she hadn't found out anything new by midnight, Dan would be on his way out of the country, forever beyond her reach.

Half inclined to delay the moment now it was actually here, Gaelle lingered over washing and dressing, and had coffee and toast sent to her room for breakfast. She could only pick at the food, feeling too keyed up to eat.

When she could delay no longer, she set off for May's house and was soon walking up the flagstoned path. But there was no response to her knock. Coupled with the unanswered phone, Gaelle began to worry. What if something had happened to May? She had told Gaelle she was widow. Perhaps she was ill.

'Are you looking for Mrs Dreyfuss, love?'

On the point of walking around to the back of the house, Gaelle paused. An elderly woman was watching her over a side fence. 'Yes, I was. I couldn't reach her by telephone and I was starting to worry.'

The woman's wariness vanished. 'That was kind of you, love. Not many would bother these days. But you've no need to worry—she's up at the church hall. The annual fête is on today, and she's been helping them get it ready.'

Relief broke over Gaelle like a wave. She had begun to fear the worst, but here was a simple explanation for May's absence, after all. After asking the neighbour for directions, she set off towards the church.

The fête was obviously a major event in the small township. It was in full swing by the time Gaelle arrived, with stalls, children carrying balloons, and wheezy music coming from a small merry-go-round outside the church grounds. Half the town must be here, Gaelle judged from the throng.

Knowing that May was helping to run the fête, Gaelle looked for her behind the numerous stalls. Finally, she spotted the woman standing behind a table of handmade baby clothes. She went up to the table. 'Hello, Mrs Dreyfuss,' she said.

'What can I do for you?' came the automatic response, then the woman's smile froze on her pale lips. 'Oh, it's you!'

Gaelle made her answering smile as disarming as she could. 'I've been trying to call you, but I see you've been busy. How's the fête going?'

'As you can see, it's doing well,' May said, but the wariness remained in her eyes.

Gaelle surveyed the piles of handmade dresses, shawls and bootees, appraising the lace trimmings with an expert eye. 'Did you make these?' she said.

Without looking at Gaelle, May shook her head. 'Oh no, dear. They were done by the Ladies' Guild.'

'Come now, May, you're much too modest,' protested a voice behind Gaelle. When she turned, the woman smiled and held out her hand. 'I'm June Allmar, the vicar's wife. The Ladies' Guild couldn't do without May. She makes the finest lace in the district. She trimmed every one of these lovely things.' When May mewed a protest, she waved her aside. 'Credit where credit's due, I say, don't you?'

Before Gaelle could formulate a reply, Mrs Allmar had been swallowed up by the crowd. Her gaze swung to May, standing helplessly behind the counter. There was a sheen of moisture in her eyes. 'We need to talk,' Gaelle said urgently.

May spread her hands wide. 'I'll be here all day.'

'I could come to your house after the fête finishes.'

'No, I . . . the vicar is having a tea for the helpers afterwards.'

'It's very important that I see you,' Gaelle insisted.

May's fingers fluttered and she folded them tightly together. Her knuckles were white, Gaelle noticed. 'There's nothing more I can tell you,' she insisted.

'Dan leaves for the Middle East at midnight tonight,' said Gaelle with seeming irrelevance. She saw the woman's hands clench even more tightly. 'He's never coming back.'

With a little gasp, May turned away and began tidying the already immaculate display behind her. 'Go away, please,' she begged.

'I don't want to distress you,' Gaelle said gently. 'But two lives, maybe three, will be ruined if I go away now.' When there was no response, she clutched at May's arm, feeling tears cloud her own eyes. 'Can't you see? I love him, May. And I'm going to lose him for ever. He'll never trust himself to love again. How can you do this to him?'

She fumbled in her handbag and brought out a

business card from her motel. 'Here's where I'm staying until tomorrow. If his happiness means anything to you, call me.'

Her heart was heavy as she turned and stumbled through the crowd, the relaxed, happy faces mocking her as she fought to control her despair, at least until she was safely back in her motel room.

The hours ticked by with agonising slowness. She ate some of the fruit she had brought with her for lunch, then threw the half-finished meal away. She was hungry, but not for food. She could hardly believe that May could be so cruel.

The throaty sound of a car pulling up outside startled her into full wakefulness. Groggily, she looked at her bedside clock. She must have dozed off, after all. Was it May whose car she had heard outside?

Hardly daring to hope, she hurried to the door and peered outside. There was only one car parked on the gravel driveway, and her heart turned over as she recognised the copper colour. 'Dan! Oh, my God, it is you!'

It was all she could do not to throw herself into his arms. He seemed to be having similar difficulty, because he took a half-step towards her, then checked himself.

'Hello, Gaelle. I didn't know you were staying here.'

So he wasn't here because of her, after all. 'Then why are you here?' she asked, disappointment souring her tone.

An expression of pain flicked across his face. 'Don't sound so unhappy—I can't bear it.'

'As you reminded me, I have no choice but to bear it,' she told him. Why had he come, when nothing had changed between them? 'Where's Gloria?' she asked, half expecting to see the other woman in his car.

Dan made a pattern in the gravel with the toe of his shoe. 'She isn't here. I came alone.'

'Why, Dan? Don't tell me you're clutching at straws too?' Even as she said it, Gaelle couldn't contain the tiny flame of hope that flickered to life inside her at the thought.

He nodded. 'I guess I am. The more I thought about Mary Taylor and the lace, the more I saw that you were right. There has to be another explanation, maybe one that makes a difference to us.' His voice broke. 'I couldn't leave knowing I might be making the greatest mistake of my life.'

'Oh, Dan!' The bitterness which was pure defence mechanism fled from her voice, and in its place was all the love she bore for him. 'I'm so glad you came! I tried to see May today, but she wouldn't talk to me. I know she's hiding something. Perhaps she'll talk to you.'

'Perhaps.'

At the interruption they spun around to find May watching them from the shelter of the pine trees. Her face was white and she clutched her handbag like a lifeline as she came towards them. When Dan turned towards her, she froze and silent tears began to roll down her cheeks. 'My God—oh my God,' she said over and over.

Gaelle took her arm and led her into the motel room. Danm followed them and shut the door, saying nothing as Gaelle helped the woman to a chair. 'Would you like some water?' she asked, although it was an effort to speak for the tightness in her throat.

May nodded. 'Please.'

She gripped the glass in a hand that shook so violently that drops of water spilled on to the carpet. Hastily she set the drink down. All the time, her eyes never left Dan, who stood with his back braced against the door, watching her.

'You're my mother, aren't you?' said Dan at last.

'Lord forgive me, yes,' she whispered. 'I never thought I'd see you again!'

'And now you have,' Dan said evenly.

May flinched as if he had struck her. 'Don't hate me, please! You have the right, but I've hated myself for so many years that I couldn't bear it if you turned against me.'

'The way you turned against me, when I was born?' he asked.

'I didn't, I swear it wasn't like that! If there'd been another way . . .' May's voice trailed away on a sob, and she clutched the back of her hand to her mouth to silence it.

Gaelle knelt beside her. Dan's coldness frightened her. She had expected almost any reaction, but not this icy indifference. Of all people, she knew the power of his passions. She wasn't going to let him retreat behind an emotionless façade, where neither she nor May could ever reach him again. Her gaze went from him to the weeping woman beside her. 'Perhaps it would be best if you started from the beginning. Why did you tell us Dan's mother was Mary Taylor?'

'Because that's my name,' May said in a despairing whisper. 'There were two of us at the same school. I was known as May to avoid confusion. Most people have forgotten my real name by now. Dreyfuss was my late husband's name.'

'But what about my father's engagement to Mary Taylor, the other one?' asked Gaelle, confused.

'Everything I told you about Simpson Maxwell and Mary was the truth,' May vowed. 'Everything except for the baby. She was going blind, but I was the one who was pregnant.'

'By my father?'

May covered her face with her hands. 'No—I made that part up. The father was another boy I was seeing. When he found out, he ran away to the Army. He was killed in an accident during his training.'

'Why did you lie about the father's name?'

May spread her hands helplessly. 'I didn't know what to do. My father was the local vicar and would have killed me if he found out how I'd disgraced him. So I kept my condition a secret and went to Sydney, supposedly for the craft exhibition, but really to have my child. After the engagement picture appeared, people kept congratulating me in mistake for Mary. So I got the idea of putting Simpson's name on the certificate. With two Mary Taylors in the town, I thought if anybody found out, they would think the other Mary was the one.'

'Which was just what happened,' said Gaelle,

letting her breath out in a rush.

'I didn't mean to hurt anyone,' May said, starting to cry again.

'Oh, no? What about the son you bore?'

Dan's harsh comment reminded them that he was still standing at the door like an avenging angel. Gaelle had never seen him look so terrifying.

She could feel May trembling under her hand, so she put an arm around the older woman. 'Dan, can't you see how upset she is?'

'Don't forget, I was the one she abandoned,' he said savagely. 'I had to endure all those years of not knowing who I was or where I came from, afraid to live a normal life for the fear of the consequences.'

'If I could have come back for you, I would,' May said piteously.

'Tell us what happened,' urged Gaelle. She prayed that May would help Dan to understand. Looking at the broken woman beside her, she couldn't believe her act had been wanton. There had to be a good reason for what she had done.

'When the baby . . . when you were born, I was very ill,' May told him. 'Very few people outside the hospital knew I'd had a child and I kept you in my room, only taking you out for walks in the early morning when no one was around.' Her voice softened. 'You were a good baby—never a cry.'

'Go on,' Dan intervened.

Hope surged in Gaelle's breast. He did want to know the truth, despite the stony façade. 'You were ill?' she prompted.

'Yes. The baby was heavy and I set him down on a seat in a bus shelter while I got my breath. Then some friends of mine came along who knew my father. They . . . I had to walk away and pretend the child wasn't mine, until they went away.' May's voice dropped to a hoarse whisper. 'When they left and I turned to get Dan, he was gone. Someone had seen him there and taken him to the police. I didn't know what to do. I thought if I claimed him, I'd be charged with some crime for leaving him, or else it would be in the papers for my father to see. I'd decided to give myself up and let them do what they liked to me, when I read that he'd been taken in by a good family.'

'The Lawsons,' Gaelle supplied.

'That's right. I read that they already had a son, so I knew my boy would have a brother and all the things I couldn't give him. It seemed as if God had made the decision for me. I went back to Bundanoon and looked after my father till he died, then I married Fred Dreyfuss.' May looked up at Dan, her eyes beseeching. 'But I never forgot you, son, not for a minute or an hour or a day. Can you ever forgive me?'

Gaelle looked at Dan in time to see the stony façade crumble completely. Without a word, he crossed the room and knelt beside May, wrapping his arms around her and burying his face against her. When he looked up, his eyes were glistening. Soundlessly, Gaelle stood up and slipped out of the room. Nothing could make up for the suffering they had endured separately, but she could at least give them a few minutes alone together.

In the midst of May's grief, she had absorbed one shining fact—Dan was not her brother, after all! There were no blood ties keeping them apart. It was the finest gift anyone had ever given her.

At last the door opened and Dan emerged, holding May's hand. 'She going home now,' he said gruffly.

May beamed. She looked years younger and her tearstained cheeks glowed. 'You will come and stay with me tomorrow?' she asked, looking anxiously up at Dan. 'I couldn't stand losing you again.'

'We'll come, first thing tomorrow,' Dan assured her. 'Gaelle and I have a lot of things to sort out first.'

'I understand.' She came to Gaelle and took both her hands, gripping them tightly. 'I don't know how I can ever repay you.'

Gaelle felt her cheeks growing hot. 'You've already repaid me amply. I don't know what I would have done if you hadn't come forward.'

'When you said two lives would be ruined, I couldn't stay away,' May confessed. 'Knowing how much I suffered after Dan was gone, I couldn't put anyone through such anguish.' She patted Gaelle's cheek. 'You're a fine person, just like your father. He never knew how I'd used his name, but somehow I don't think he would have blamed me.'

'I'm sure he wouldn't,' said Gaelle softly.

They watched May until she was out of sight, then Dan pulled Gaelle into the circle of his arms. His lips nuzzled her hairline. 'How I've longed to do this!' he breathed. 'I love you so much.'

She moulded herself against him. 'I love you too.'
She smiled up at him. 'It feels good to be able to say it
and not feel guilt-stricken.'

Dan nodded. 'You know, even when I believed it
was wrong, I couldn't stop myself loving you.'

Her heart sang. 'And now I wouldn't want you
to.'

He pulled her into the motel room and closed the
door, then sought her mouth in a hungry kiss that
told her how much he had been holding back.

As she returned his kiss Gaelle felt her heartbeat
gather speed and heat flooded through her. With a
need born of desperation, she clung to him, aware of
how close she had come to losing him. He sensed her
fear and his hands tightened across her back,
drawing her against him so she could feel his
answering need.

Their eyes did all the talking as they pulled apart
and began to shed their clothes. Gaelle feasted her
eyes on Dan's magnificent body, longing to run her
hands up and down his lean hardness. She
restrained herself until they lay stretched out on the
narrow bed, then she gave herself up to her need to
touch and told him.

Much later, she lay in the crook of his arm, content to
listen to his even breathing and feel his body pressed
against hers.

Tilting her head, she was surprised to find that he
wasn't asleep but was watching her, a look of lazy
satiety on his face. 'What are you looking so pleased
about?' she asked.

Dan's smile widened as he regarded her with such

love that her heart felt as if it would explode. 'You mean as if you didn't know?' She began to protest, but he kissed her into silence. 'I was just wondering how many afternoons we can arrange to spend like this after we're married.'

'You mean *if* we marry,' said Gaelle in mock outrage. 'You haven't asked me yet.'

'Do I have to?'

'No,' she admitted. 'I've already said yes in every way I know.'

'We'll make it soon. Scott will love being best man.'

'He'll like that,' she agreed, 'although he only wants me in the family as fodder for his show.'

'I don't mind how you spend your time, as long as I have first claim,' Dan said.

There was no contest. 'First, last and always,' she vowed.

He clasped his hands behind his head. 'I've been thinking, I shall have to find a safer occupation.'

'But you love your work. I wouldn't dream of asking you to make such a sacrifice.'

He shook his head. 'It's no sacrifice. I want to do it. Taking risks was fine when I had nothing to lose. Now, I have too much at stake. Besides, I enjoyed doing the computer programming. I might do more of that.'

Leaning across him, Gaelle planted a loving kiss on his half-open mouth. 'Whatever you want to do is fine with me.'

Dan's eyes sparkled with delight. 'I hope you mean that, because I know what I want to do right now.' Then his arms came around her again and he pulled her on top of him. There was no doubt about what he had in mind. She nibbled provocatively at his full lower lip, sending waves of sensation shooting through them both. 'Start as you mean to go on, I say,' she murmured.

So they did.

Harlequin Presents

Coming Next Month

Available in January wherever paperback books are sold, or through Harlequin Reader Service:

In the U.S.
901 Fuhrmann Blvd.
P.O. Box 1397
Buffalo, N.Y. 14240-1397

In Canada
P.O. Box 603
Fort Erie, Ontario
L2A 5X3

CHRISTMAS IS FOR KIDS

Spend this holiday season with nine very special children. Children whose wishes come true at the magical time of Christmas.

Read American Romance's CHRISTMAS IS FOR KIDS— heartwarming holiday stories in which children bring together four couples who fall in love. Meet:

Frank, Dorcas, Kathy, Candy and Nicky—They become friends at St. Christopher's orphanage, but they really want to be adopted and become part of a real family, in #321 *A Carol Christmas* by Muriel Jensen.

Patty—She's a ten-year-old certified genius, but she wants what every little girl wishes for: a daddy of her own, in #322 *Mrs. Scrooge* by Barbara Bretton.

Amy and Flash—Their mom is about to deliver their newest sibling any day, but Christmas just isn't the same now—not without their dad. More than anything they want their family reunited for Christmas, in #323 *Dear Santa* by Margaret St. George.

Spencer—Living with his dad and grandpa in an all-male household has its advantages, but Spence wants Santa to bring him a mommy to love, in #324 *The Best Gift of All* by Andrea Davidson.

These children will win your hearts as they entice—and matchmake—the adults into a true romance. This holiday, invite them—and the four couples they bring together—into your home.

Look for all four CHRISTMAS IS FOR KIDS books available now from Harlequin American Romance. And happy holidays!

XMAS-KIDS-1R

Wonderful, luxurious gifts can be yours with proofs-of-purchase from any specially marked "Indulge A Little" Harlequin or Silhouette book with the Offer Certificate properly completed, plus a check or money order (do not send cash) to cover postage and handling payable to Harlequin/Silhouette "Indulge A Little, Give A Lot" Offer. We will send you the specified gift.

Mail-in-Offer

OFFER CERTIFICATE

Item	A. Collector's Doll	B. Soaps in a Basket	C. Potpourri Sachet	D Scented Hangers
# of Proofs-of-Purchase	18	12	6	4
Postage & Handling	$3.25	$2.75	$2.25	$2.00
Check One				

Name _____

Address _____ Apt. # ____

City _____ State _____ Zip _____

Indulge
A LITTLE
GIVE A LOT

ONE PROOF OF PURCHASE

To collect your free gift by mail you must include the necessary number of proofs-of-purchase plus postage and handling with offer certificate.

HP-3

Harlequin®/Silhouette®

Mail this certificate, designated number of proofs-of-purchase and check or money order for postage and handling to:

INDULGE A LITTLE
P.O. Box 9055
Buffalo, N.Y. 14269-9055